£1·50

All the

Walker Hamilton was born in 1954 at Airdrie, Lanark-
shire. His father was a coal-miner, and from him he
inherited a love of books. He left school at fifteen, and
did general office work, studying accountancy at evening
classes, until his national service in the RAF, most of
which was spent in a military hospital in Scotland. He
was discharged on medical grounds after a severe illness.
He then worked in a Glasgow brewery, followed by a
spell as an office-machine mechanic, after which he had
a variety of unskilled manual jobs. He married in 1960,
and died in February 1969. This, his first novel, was first
published in 1968.

WALKER HAMILTON

All the Little Animals

INDIGO

First published in Great Britain 1968
by Victor Gollancz Ltd

This Indigo edition published 1998
Indigo is an imprint of the Cassell Group
Wellington House, 125 Strand, London WC2R 0BB

Copyright © Walker Hamilton 1968

A catalogue record for this book is
available from the British Library.

ISBN 0 575 40186 9

Printed and bound in Great Britain by
Guernsey Press Co. Ltd, Guernsey, Channel Isles

2 4 6 8 10 9 7 5 3 1

Contents

for Dorothy

1: The Little Man

I can remember the tune, not the name of it, because I'm no good at names, but the sound of it. I'll never forget the sound of that tune. I can't remember the driver-man's face though, and that's funny really, because I watched him as he died and yet his face is just nothing under black hair in my memory. Poor driver-man.

He didn't speak much to me as we ran west through the rain. Perhaps he regretted having given me a lift, or maybe he was just tired. I was tired. I was tired and happy and afraid. All at once? Yes. I was tired because I had been travelling all night and hadn't eaten anything since last night's supper, and I was happy to be away from the Fat. I was afraid in case they would come after me and find me, afraid of the Fat.

It was all magicky – is that a word? – it was magic then, in Cornwall I mean. I could feel the magic pulling the big lorry west and my head was full of light and the radio music was tinkly – is that a word? – it tinkled like – like glass bells. It was a magic music. His overalls smelled funny. Not nice, but not bad, just funny. I'd never smelled that smell before, in fact I'd never been in a lorry before, or in Cornwall, or – anywhere.

I saw the rabbit first. A real rabbit, and I was just going to say, 'Look, a rabbit,' when he laughed and for a moment I laughed with him until I knew what he was going to do. He had big, knobbly, dirty hands which twisted the lorry so that it would crush the rabbit, and he was laughing.

We swung on to the rabbit and I wanted to shout, 'Run! Run!' because it just crouched there and never moved when it could have run away. I felt the little bump and then the funny gliding feeling, and then the driver-man stopped laughing.

Everything was so *slow*.

Ahead there was a humpy stone bridge which was bending towards us very slowly and the driver-man was swearing and the lorry was screeching just as if it was alive. He didn't like the screeching. His face got all twisted and wrong just like the way the Fat's face used to go when the hate bubbled up in him. Only with the driver-man it wasn't hate, it was fear.

After that it was all big, slow bangs until I was lying with my face in the grass. The grass was wet and I could only see out of one eye because of the way I was lying. I could see a wheel spinning and bits of broken glass everywhere and I was afraid because it was so still after the loudness except for the music. It was raining a little bit and I liked the feel of it on my skin. Then there was the frightening noise and I scrambled up quickly. I was awful dizzy and I thought I would cry, but I couldn't. Then I was afraid I was hurt and I felt myself all over, but I was all right. I was all dirty, but I didn't have any really sore places.

The driver-man had sore places, and he was making the noises. Bubbly noises. He was all torn, not just his clothes, his *self*. He was lying on the grass with his arms and legs all twisted about, but his eyes were open and he was looking at me. You're supposed to go and help people when there's been an accident. That was what it was you see, an *accident*, and I *was* going to help him until I saw the little man.

I couldn't see him very well, because it was still almost night-time and the sky was just beginning to look like grey-glass. But I could hear him. He said: 'Leave him alone,' and his voice was little too. Not like the Fat's voice which was big and heavy and frightening just like the Fat himself. The little man's voice was squeaky and tiny, and he was so little I would have thought it wasn't a man at all but just a schoolboy, only he had a man's clothes on and specs and he didn't stand like a boy. He stooped, and besides, you could smell he was old.

I stopped when he said to and then I noticed that he was holding something in his arms.

'What have you got?' I said. He didn't answer me. He didn't even look at me, just stood looking at the driver-man and listening to the noises he was making.

'There's been an accident,' I said, and he looked at me then. It was getting lighter quickly now and his specs were shiny like two silver pennies where his eyes should have been.

I said: 'You're supposed to help people when there's been an accident,' then I went closer to see what he was holding.

'It's a rabbit,' he said.

I like rabbits so I went really close to him. I told him I liked rabbits and asked if I could touch it, but he didn't answer me. I did touch the rabbit and it was hard and cold, not like a rabbit should be. I didn't like it and snatched my hand away.

'What's the matter with it?' I said.

'It's dead, boy,' he murmured, 'it's dead.'

The driver-man was making awful noises now and I said: 'You're supposed to help people when there's been –'

'Be quiet, boy,' the little man said. 'You only help good people. That man is a bad man. He killed this rabbit.'

I remembered then. 'Yes. Yes I know. I was with him when he did it.' The driver-man's eyes were shouting at me so I looked away from him. He was a bad man. The little man sat down on an old, broken tree which lay near the stream and I sat beside him. Apart from the radio, which was still playing where it lay in the wet grass, and the noises the driver-man was making, it was very nice and quiet by the stream. The trees were green. I mean the trunks as well as the leaves. They were smeared with green slimy stuff and the hollow we were in was damp. I could feel it through my trousers where I sat. I could just see the road and the humpy bridge through the trees and the road was empty. There was a broken bit on the humpy bridge and big stones lay scattered around. That was because of the accident you see.

The stream wasn't very big but it ran fast, bubbling over stones which had the same green stuff on them as the tree trunks. I watched the water for a long time until the driver-man's noises got less and less and then stopped altogether.

The little man laid the rabbit down very gently on the grass and went over to look at the driver-man. I came beside him and he said: 'He's like the rabbit now.'

'Dead you mean?'

'Dead.'

'You're supposed to bury dead people,' I said.

'His own kind can bury him,' said the little man.

He took a step nearer the radio and kicked it into the stream. 'His own stinking kind can do it, boy. I have other work.' The radio plopped into the stream, but I could still see it, all silvery and blue, and it still played. In the *water*. That was funny. Music coming out of the *water*. I laughed and the little man turned to look at me. There was sunlight now and the silver pennies were back over his eyes. He looked at me for a long time, then he said: 'How old are you, boy?'

I liked it when he called me boy. I'm not a boy really, that's what my mother used to say, I'm thirty-one years old, but I like to be called boy. Maybe it's because all the years went quicker for me than for ordinary people, I'm not ordinary, and I'm not really a boy. I'm thirty-one. A man I suppose, but I *feel* like a boy.

I told the little man I was thirty-one. I expected him to be like all the others and look at me as if I wasn't really there, as if I couldn't see their eyes, as if it didn't matter if *I* could see *their* eyes. But he only nodded and turned away. He picked up a small rucksack which I hadn't noticed before and slung it on his shoulder, then he gathered up the rabbit in his arms and walked quickly away through the trees.

I followed him as quietly as I could but the crackling of twigs under my feet gave me away and he knew I was there all right, but he never looked round or spoke. He walked in the funniest way with his knees bent and his head down, a kind of stumble which carried him over the ground quickly so that I was out of breath when he stopped. The silver pennies flashed at me and I stayed where I was, a few yards from him. We were in a lane with high banks on either side and spiky bushes with yellow flowers like candle-flames on them, and even though the sun had got brighter it was a shadow-place and I was almost afraid. But then I thought to myself that I wasn't afraid of anything except the Fat, so it was all right really.

The little man put the rabbit on the bank and slipped the rucksack from his shoulder. I wanted to see what he was going to do so I went a bit closer. He looked at me again without smiling, but he didn't say not to come so I went right up to him. He took a trowel, a garden trowel, out of the rucksack and began to dig in the bottom of the bank. The soil was nearly black and when I took some in my fingers it was crumbly and soft. His trowel was green, green metal, and I watched as it slid in and out of the cool earth until he had dug quite a big hole. He put his trowel down then and lifted the rabbit and laid it in the hole. Then he covered it up with earth and arranged the turf so that nobody would ever know that there was a rabbit down there. He had buried it.

He put his trowel away in the rucksack, slung the rucksack on his shoulder and began to walk away down the lane. I hurried along at his side.

'Why did you do that?' I said.

He turned his head to look at me and in the shadows there were no silver pennies. He had grey eyes, the grey bit so pale that it almost didn't show up against the white. I'd never seen eyes like that before. My eyes are brown.

'You mean why did I bury the creature?' he said.

'Yes.'

'Because it was dead, boy,' he said. 'And because I wanted to. There's a – satisfaction in burying things.'

I didn't know what to say, so I didn't say anything at all. I was angry with myself for not knowing what to say, because people don't often talk to me. Not *talk*, they just say stupid, kindly things and don't listen to me or answer my questions. We walked for a long time and it was nice. After the dark lane there were other lanes, some bright and some shadowed, but always with the high banks on each side and the green and yellow bushes, and sometimes crooked little trees grew on top of the banks.

Then suddenly we were on a road and he began to hurry. It was a narrow road and when a car passed we had to walk in single file. The little man muttered angrily whenever a car or a lorry swept past us, but he never once spoke to me or looked at me even, and when he turned abruptly off the road I nearly lost him. I clambered through the gap in the bank where he had disappeared just in time to see him vanish through a thick clump of the green and yellow bushes. I hurried across the little field and pushed through behind him. The bushes were very prickly and hard to get past, but I managed it and came to a place which had been a track a long time ago but now was covered with grass and nettles. The trees and bushes hung over it so that it was like a green cave and the little man was sitting in the green cave, sitting on the grass under a greyish tree which crouched over him like a hand or a wing. He had taken off his rucksack and was taking things out of it and laying them around him. After spreading a yellow cycle cape on the ground, he set out two tin cups and a big thermos flask. There was a little flat bottle of whisky and a packet of biscuits as well.

I noticed his hands then for the first time. They were very small and slender, with delicate fingers and long nails. His hands were the opposite of his face which was unshaven and wrinkly all over. His clothes were just clothes, an old mac, a cloth cap and worn shoes. It was then that I realised he was watching me, watching me even as I was staring at him. He was a funny little man. The more you looked at him the less you could see. He was camouflaged. I mean his *self* was camouflaged, and sometimes you could see him behind his specs and sometimes the silver pennies were there and the little man was gone again.

Invisible.

I could feel that my mouth was open, so I closed it. Mother used to always be telling me not to go about with my mouth open. That's one of the things I do you see, I can't help it. I just forget.

'I'm sorry,' I said. 'I didn't mean to be rude. I know you're not supposed to stare at people.'

'Sit down, boy,' he said. 'I'm having tea. Are you hungry?'

I was awful hungry. 'Yes.'

He took a biscuit for himself and gave me the packet. 'Eat all you want, boy.' He unscrewed the top of the thermos flask and poured tea into the tin cups and added sugar from a paper packet. 'No milk, I'm afraid,' he said, 'but it's sweet and hot.' He put quite a lot of whisky from the flat bottle into his own tea, but none into mine. I'd never had tea from a tin cup before and it was warm and friendly in my hands. I ate several biscuits and then I just *had* to ask him.

'Excuse me,' I said.

He looked at me.

'Why did you bury the rabbit?'

'I told you already, boy, because it was dead, and because I wanted to. That's why.' He poured out more tea for both of us. 'And besides,' he went on, 'it's my work.'

I tried to think quickly what I would say next, because I wanted him to keep talking to me. I don't often have conversations with people, but it was all right, he went on without me having to speak.

'Rabbits,' he murmured, 'are generally considered to be *nice* things.' I nodded. He was right, rabbits *are* nice things.

'And rats are generally detested,' he said. 'But both are living creatures and when they are killed they should be buried.'

'That's right,' I said. 'You're supposed to bury dead *people*.'

'People can bury each other, boy,' he said crossly, 'but the animals have to be helped. Not just rabbits and rats, but *all* the little animals, boy.' He sighed. 'Other men kill them and I bury them. I bury rats and mice and birds and hedgehogs and frogs and even snails.' He nibbled a biscuit. 'Of course I don't really bury snails, but I take the remains off the road and drop them in high grass or nettles. Out of sight, you see, boy, out of sight.'

16

My mouth was open again.

'You'll find that your tea will get cold more quickly out of doors,' he said. 'I should drink up if I were you. Another biscuit?'

I was still hungry, because biscuits aren't much really, but I was so excited about what he said that I couldn't be bothered with my stupid stomach. 'Excuse me,' I said, 'but where do you find so many things to bury? – and who kills them?'

He had only a small face, with a pointed chin, but now it screwed up in anger and he looked really fierce.

'On the roads, boy, the high-roads and the by-roads, where the wheels are, boy, and the men behind the wheels. They drive their silly metal boxes and kill and kill and KILL –'

He frightened me. Some of my tea spilled and I felt it warm on my leg, then he grabbed my arm. 'I've buried so many, boy, so *many*.' His hand on my arm was trembling and the shaking from him came through me.

'You must know, boy. You must have been in cars, must have felt the odd little bump, the faint crunch under your wheels. *Must* have boy. You must have had the tiny choice cross your mind as a little blob of something alive showed up in the headlights and you drove on and over it and forgot about it. You must have cursed when the body of a small bird banged on the precious paintwork of your bloody car, ey?'

His voice was loud now and he was shaking me by the arm. A fleck of white had come to each corner of his thin lips. His lips were very thin. 'How many have you killed, boy? And why? WHY?'

I began to cry and he let me go. 'Stop crying now, boy. Have some more tea.'

I tried to stop crying. 'Excuse me,' I said, 'but I don't – can't drive a car.'

'Oh.'

'And I've never killed things.'

'Then I'm sorry, boy,' he said. 'You must forgive me, I don't often have company.'

We were quiet for a while then and he packed up all the things in his bag and lit a cigarette. The tea had made me feel sleepy and cosy and I closed my eyes. I was really tired, and I remember thinking that the yellow flowers on the prickly bushes were more like little Dutch shoes than candle-flames.

When I opened my eyes again he wasn't there. I didn't know which way to go, but I took a chance and ran up the green cave until I came out into the sunlight. I was on a narrow road and I was lucky, I just caught a glimpse of the little man as he turned into another lane. My legs were stinging from the nettles and I tore my jacket on a gate I had to climb over. There was barbed wire along the top bar of that gate. Why do people put that stuff on gates? Cows can't climb over gates, can they? Anyway, I ran as fast as I could and caught up with the little man.

'Hello,' I said, all out of breath, 'I was sleeping.'

He turned to face me but I couldn't see his eyes.

'What do you want now, boy?' he said, and his voice wasn't very friendly.

'I want to come with you.'

'Go home, boy, you can't come with me.'

'I can't go home,' I said. 'I've run away.'

He shifted the weight of his rucksack. 'Well, I can't take you with me. I have work to do.' He turned away and walked quickly on up the lane. I ran beside him.

'I could help you with the work,' I suggested. 'I *want* to help you.' That stopped him. The stubble on his chin rasped under his fingers, and I thought it would be all right, but then he shook his head.

'No good, boy. I don't know you. You say you've run away?'

I nodded.

'Police might come. I don't want to talk to police – to anyone.'

'I could carry your rucksack.'

'No.'

'Excuse me, but I could make the tea – I think.'

'No.'

'Or I could help with the digging –'

'Go home, boy!' he shouted suddenly. 'Go away!'

'But I haven't got anything to *do*!' I cried. 'All I want is something to *do*.'

My face was going away from me then, the way it does sometimes, and I could feel my eyes opening and shutting bang-bang-bang and the tears all hot running down the river-beds they've gradually made for themselves. Thirty-one years is quite a long time, and I've cried a lot. I began to think that maybe the little man was right, and maybe the police might come and get me and take me back to the Fat. How I hated the Fat, and the smell of the Fat. I didn't hate anything or anybody else, just the Fat. Some things I don't *like*, but that's different. I don't like wet feet, but I don't hate them either. I cried and cried until I fell down and the little man picked me up again.

He made the usual noises that people make when I cry too much and after a while I felt a bit better. When I could speak I said: 'Can I come with you?'

He didn't say no this time but he didn't say I could go with him either. We walked on much more slowly than before, and my face came back to where I could make it do what I wanted. He stopped and put his hand on my arm.

'Do you really want to help me with the work, boy?'

'Yes,' I said. 'Oh, yes please.'

'And do you like animals? *All* the little animals?'

'Yes, yes,' I said. 'I love the animals.'

He rubbed his noisy bristles again and sighed. 'All right, boy. You can come to work with me.'

I don't think I've ever been so happy as when the little man said that. At least, not since Mother died. I wanted to thank him but I didn't know how to say it.

'I'm going to give you a test, boy,' he said. He took the trowel from his rucksack and gave it to me. 'There,' he said, and pointed. I couldn't see it at first, because I'd been crying you see and my eyes weren't working properly yet, but I walked a few paces ahead and looked at the spot he was pointing to. I saw it then. I wanted to do well in my test, but this was – a rat.

But it didn't look like a rat, it didn't look like anything. It was just a reddish-brown and grey mess squashed down into the stony soil of the lane. It was as if it had been stamped and stamped into the ground until it was just a flat, hairy nothing. And it stank. The only thing about it that looked like a rat was the tail. The tail was all right.

I knew the little man was behind me, watching, so I had to do it. The flies buzzed up when I came close and startled me and I dropped the trowel, but I picked it up again and began digging in the bank and soon I had a hole big enough. That was the easy part, I don't know how I did the rest. Just sort of scraped it up.

'That's good, boy,' he said, and took the trowel from me. He got a piece of newspaper from the rucksack and struck a match to it, then he put the burning paper on the ground and held the blade of the trowel in the flames.

'This is to clean the trowel, boy, can you remember that?'

'I'll remember,' I said.

'There are other things you have to remember,' he said sternly. 'Now listen, boy. One. You must never talk to anyone about the work or about me. Two. You must always do as I say.' He put his face close to mine and I could smell the tobacco from his mouth. 'And three. You must never kill anything, boy. Do you understand that? Never kill anything.'

'I'll remember them all,' I said. 'I promise.' It was inside my head that there was one thing I would like to kill, but I kept the thought there, away inside in the dark places and I didn't tell the little man. And then I was happy. I was so happy I wanted to dance.

'What do we do now?' I asked him.

'We have things to buy for you.'

That was exciting. 'What things,' I shouted, 'tell me what things?'

'The things you are going to need for the work. What's your name, boy?'

'Bobby.'

'You can call me Mr. Summers, boy.'

'Yes, Mr. Summers.'

'But you must never tell anyone what my name is. That's one more thing for you to remember.'

'I'll never tell. But –'

'Yes?'

'Why don't you want anyone to know your name, Mr. Summers? Are you afraid of somebody?'

He was quiet for a while, then he said: 'There's another thing to remember, boy. Don't ask too many questions.'

'I'm sorry. Is it all right to ask questions about the work?'

'Yes. Yes, that's all right, boy. Now come on.'

Mr. Summers knew where he was going, but I would have been lost in five minutes with all the twists and turns we made. It was tiring and I was glad when we came out on to a main road by a bus stop. The bus came almost at once, and we got on and sat upstairs so Mr. Summers could smoke. After he paid the fares he didn't speak much, he looked nervous, and I could see he hated being on the bus so I didn't bother him with questions.

It took us an hour to reach the town, and it was only a small place, not like where I come from. The place I come from is a city. The shops weren't very good in the town, not like Mother's store. The store. It should be my store really, all five floors. You can get anything in Mother's store. There are departments for food and tools and clothes and – well, everything. It's a department store, and there's even a pet department. I liked it best. All that should be mine really, because my Mother is dead now and my Father died a long time ago, so it should be mine. But the Fat took it away, and anyway, I'm not clever enough to have a store. I'm not clever enough for anything really I suppose. Except the work.

'We'll go in here first, boy,' Mr. Summers said.

It was a camping shop. I got a blue sleeping bag and a small rucksack like the one Mr. Summers had. Then we went to another shop and he bought me a trowel. My trowel was like his except that it was painted red. I told him I was still hungry and he took me to a café where we had egg and chips and bread and butter and tea. Then we went out again and Mr. Summers got run over by a car. Well, he wasn't really run over, that's just what people always say. Mr. Summers was knocked over, not run over. The car bumped him and he just fell down. But it was awful for a while, because his face went so white I thought he was dead. Dead people go white.

As I bent down to help him I could feel him shaking all over so I knew it was going to be all right. A lot of people came to look, but Mr. Summers got up and told me to hurry away and not speak to anyone. We bought lots of food and tobacco and a bottle of whisky for Mr. Summers, and then we went to the bus place.

I was glad to get on the bus, because I didn't like that town. It was full of people all bigger than us who always seemed to be trying to push us off the pavement. Going back to the lanes was like going home again.

I don't know where we got off the bus, but we walked a long way and it began to get dark. I would have been afraid if Mr. Summers hadn't been with me. We were getting near the sea. I could smell it and hear it, but I wasn't afraid of the sea, it was the dark. We seemed to be walking farther and deeper into the night with every step and I wished we could turn round and walk the other way, back into the light again. I know you can't do that, but I wanted to just the same.

The sea-sound got louder and we began to drop down-hill towards it till we came to a place with lots of the flat-topped trees. The track was very stony and I tripped once or twice and nearly fell until Mr. Summers brought out a small pocket torch and shone it for me. We turned off to the left, still going downhill in the dark, and on to a much narrower path, a muddy one this time with the trees and bushes growing so close on each side that we had to go in single file.

The wind had blown up now, a cold wind with the smell of the sea in it, and as we went on I heard a strange noise. It was a sound which would have made me feel awful lonely if Mr. Summers hadn't been there in front of me with his torch. Just as I was going to ask him what it was that made the noise he gave a sigh, a happy kind of sigh, and the torch lit up a broken wooden gate at the end of the path. It was then that I saw what made this strange noise, it grew on each side of the gate in high, thick clumps so that you could never have seen through it even in the daytime. But I still didn't know what it was, and as we went through the gate I asked Mr. Summers what it was. He said it was bamboo.

Bamboo.

I knew what that was all right. There are things made of it in Mother's store, but I'd never seen it growing before. I always thought it came from foreign places, far-away places, and there it was growing in Cornwall.

I reached out to touch it and it was hard and smooth and cool. It swayed all the time in the wind and clashed and rubbed to make the noise. I began to like that noise.

It was too dark to see much, but I knew we were passing through a kind of garden and then we came to a house. A hut. It was a hut, not a house. Wooden and small and hidden away behind the bamboo and the trees. I heard him unlock the door and we went inside and shut out the cold wind and the night, but I could still hear the bamboo.

Mr. Summers lit an oil lamp and there was another new thing for me. He lit another one, and the light was better than electric, nice and soft and friendly. Next he lit a paraffin stove to make us warm and soon there was a lovely, cosy, smell from the lamps and the stove and I was very happy to be in that little hut. There was one big room, the one we were in, and one tiny room which was the kitchen and the store. In the big room there were two iron beds with mattresses and pillows but no blankets or sheets. There was a table and two chairs and the floor was bare wooden planks which creaked when I stepped on it. Apart from the stove and heavy curtains at the windows there was nothing else in the room at all.

He took my rucksack from me and put it beside his on the table, then he unpacked all the food and put it in the cupboard. All except the whisky which he put on the table. He spread the sleeping bags out on the beds. His bag was green and mine was blue and they looked very nice, but mine was much brighter looking than his.

'Do you want supper, boy?' he asked.

'Yes, please,' I said, because I was still quite hungry.

I followed him into the kitchen, but there wasn't much there except a sink and a big yellow jug full of water, and another cupboard. He got a primus stove out of the cupboard and a kettle and plates and things.

We had baked beans out of a tin for supper with bread and butter, and I had tea out of the tin cup and Mr. Summers had whisky out of a glass. Afterwards we cleared the things away and he had a smoke and some more whisky. Then he said it was time for bed. He went to the cupboard and put the whisky and what was left of the food away, and brought back some cheese. We had bought a lot of cheese in town and now he took some of it and crumbled it into little heaps away from the beds. I asked him what it was for and he said it was for the mice.

Mice!

I remembered things and felt like laughing and crying at the same time.

'Are you all right, boy?' he asked. He must have been watching my face.

'Yes,' I said. 'I'm all right, Mr. Summers. Do you feed the mice every night?'

'Every night that I'm here,' he said. 'If I feed them they

don't have to steal from me. People usually kill mice when they don't want them to steal, boy, but I feed them. I'm going to put out the lamps now. Time to go to bed. Goodnight, boy.'

'Goodnight, Mr. Summers.'

The sleeping bag wasn't very warm at first, but soon I could feel it swell and tighten and then it was almost too warm. As I lay waiting to sleep I could hear Mr. Summers breathing and the wind in the bamboo and the mice. I hoped they were enjoying the cheese, and I thought about the mouse Peter.

If the mouse Peter had been there they might have made him the King or something. The mouse Peter was beautiful.

2: Me

I'd better tell you about the mouse Peter and the Fat and me, then you'll know you see.

Me first. I am thirty-one years old and my name is Bobby Platt. I was hurt by a motor-car when I was only little and I haven't been well ever since then. I can't remember about the motor-car, I'm just telling you what my Mother told me. My Father was killed a long time ago and I've never had any brothers or sisters. I used to live with my Mother until she died, then I had to live with the Fat, but I ran away.

Mother met the Fat about two years ago at a time when she was very worried about the store. She was worried because people weren't buying enough things from the store and business was bad. She gave the Fat an important job there and he *made* the people buy more things and Mother stopped worrying and was a lot happier. I don't know how he made people buy more things if they didn't want to, but he did.

It was good at first, because Mother spent a lot more time with me instead of always being at the office in the store and coming home with a headache. But then she got married to the Fat and that was bad. That was awful, because it meant that the Fat came to live at our house.

The Fat wasn't really his name of course, but I never thought of him as anything but just the Fat. He was enormous and he seemed to get bigger all the time. He had several chins and a thin nose like a knife-blade and blue eyes which were so blue that they hurt to look at. The Fat bought a lot of suits but none ever fitted him properly, the trouble was that he kept getting bigger and bursting through the suits. They were black suits, always a black suit and a white shirt and a black tie. I don't know why my Mother married him. He killed my Mother. Oh, I don't mean that he murdered her or anything, but he killed her just the same.

He shouted her to death. I used to hear him shouting at her when I was in bed at night. When Mother married the Fat she was nice and slim, but afterwards she got thinner and thinner until she just died. I watched her dying and I saw how the Fat got fatter as she got thinner. He killed her all right.

The Fat either killed things or made them go away. He made our nice housekeeper go away after Mother died and another woman came. She was called a nurse-housekeeper. Then he made Doctor Forest go away, even though Doctor Forest was making me better gradually by just talking to me. You have to be very clever to make people better by just talking to them. Like Jesus almost. But the Fat stopped Doctor Forest from coming to see me and the nurse-housekeeper was supposed to look after me. She wasn't clever at all, all she did was give me the meals that didn't taste of anything and pills that made me feel sleepy.

Our house was full of animals until the Fat killed them all. He took Maisie the cat and got her killed, and Flo the sheepdog and my pet mice and even the canaries and even the goldfish. I saw him killing the goldfish. He took them to the lavatory and emptied them into the bowl and pulled the chain.

I cried most of the time after the animals had gone.

I know he would have liked to kill me as well, but he was afraid to do that. He was going to send me away though, away to a hospital. I heard him talking to a strange Doctor about it one day when he came home from the store. They came into my room and looked at me and talked about me as if I wasn't there, not like Mother and Doctor Forest used to do, they were always nice. The strange Doctor gave me pills which made me feel sleepier than ever until all I did was lie in bed in my room and cry, and when I cried the strange Doctor or the nurse-housekeeper gave me more pills which put me to sleep.

But there were times when I didn't cry, times when they left me alone and I could remember things.

Things like going to the park with the dog and Mother. Or Mother and me and Doctor Forest playing a game called Monopoly which I never quite learned properly, but which was good fun. Most of all I used to think about the store. Platt's. That was the name in big red letters above the main door. My Mother's name. My name. Our store.

Mother used to take me there about once a week and we'd go through all the departments and I'd smile and say hallo to everybody and they'd smile and say hallo back and call me Mr. Robert. Thinking those things and remembering helped me to fight the pills which the nurse-housekeeper gave me. I tried holding them in my mouth under my tongue until she'd gone away, then I spat them out. But she must have spied on me because she got very angry and the Fat came and he was angry. He slapped me on the face and made me cry and then I got more pills. After that the nurse-housekeeper was very careful to see that I swallowed the pills. I think she was afraid of the Fat too.

The only thing I had left was a mouse. The mouse Peter. He was the only one of all my pets that I had been able to save, and I kept him in a sweet-tin at the back of my cupboard. I made air-holes for him to breathe and I put a hanky in so that he would have a nice soft bed. I saved bits of the no-food that the nurse-housekeeper gave me and fed him on that. I don't think he liked it any more than I did, but it kept him alive.

The mouse Peter was beautiful. He was white and brown and black, and he liked me, he was my secret. As long as I knew he was there in the room with me I could hold on and hope that it would all come right again like it was before. Even though he was hidden away in the sweet-tin at the back of the cupboard I could *feel* him there, and I knew the mouse Peter was with *me*, not with the nurse-housekeeper or the Fat, and I kept my secret to myself and fought the pills.

I wished a lot of things. I wished my Mother would come back and take me to the store like she used to. I know that was silly, because dead people can't come back just because you wish them to. Even clever people like Doctor Forest can't make dead people come back again. And sometimes I wished that one of the men or women from the store would come and get me, but that was no good either, the Fat had the store and he would frighten them into obeying him. The Fat could even frighten Mr. Whiteside, the floorwalker who was always so nice to me. I used to wish the Fat would die, then I could go to the store and make Mr. Whiteside the manager and I could just stay at home and he would make the store run all right, because he's very clever and never gets excited like me.

I used to wish all these things, and at times when I knew it was safe I'd take the mouse Peter out of his hiding place and into bed with me. He was so tame that he would sit in the palm of my hand while I fed him and told him all the things I was wishing about. But the weeks went by and the pills went on and none of my wishes came true.

Nobody from the store came to see me, though they must have known I was ill. Once before when I was ill they sent me a big get well card, the window-dresser had made it and it was as big as me nearly and had all their names on it. But that was a long time ago before the Fat came. The store people used to call me Mr. Robert, and my Mother used to call me Bobby, but the Fat called me stupid.

He would say: 'Hallo, stupid,' in his big, frightening voice and blow cigar smoke in my eyes. He always had a big cigar in his mouth and I think he used the cigars so that he could hide his eyes behind the smoke and people wouldn't really be able to see what he was like.

He would say: 'Hallo, stupid. It won't be long now before you get put away.' He would blow the smoke and say: 'You're going where you won't be a bother to anyone, you thick headed idiot. Your mother was an idiot and she bred you and you're a bloody looney!' He would laugh then and jab me with his finger, not play-jabs, but hard jabs that hurt me till I cried. And sometimes he'd walk about the room and swear and get angrier and angrier until finally he'd come over to the bed and slap me and slap me . . .

I know why he hated me so much, it was because I was *alive*. You see, he had the store, but he couldn't have it completely until I was dead or put away in a hospital for ever, because it said: PLATT'S, in big red letters above the door and my name was Platt and his wasn't and that made him angry. He couldn't change the name because of the law. Nobody can go against the law, everybody knows that. So I held on against the pills because I had the law and the mouse Peter on my side. He tried to get me to sign papers several times, but I remembered what my Mother had told me about signing papers and I wouldn't do it. I wouldn't sign no matter how much he slapped me, and I wouldn't sign when he was sly and called me Bobby and brought me sweets. I didn't eat the sweets in case they were poisoned.

Then one night he found my secret.

It was late and I had the mouse Peter on the pillow beside me. I was talking to him when the Fat burst into my room and switched on the light. I tried to hide the mouse Peter but the Fat saw what I was doing and slapped me and twisted my arm until he got my hand open. He grabbed the mouse Peter and held it in his fist with just its head showing at the top. I hoped the mouse Peter would bite his thumb, but I had tamed it too much.

'Well, well, well,' the Fat said. 'So this is Bobby's little friend is it?'

The Fat's hands were horrible. They were white and thick with hair on the backs of the fingers, and there always seemed to be more than four fingers and a thumb on each hand. There seemed to be as many fingers on each hand as a spider has legs, and all flashing with gold rings. But I know that couldn't have been right, it must have been the pills that made me see so many fingers.

'Does Bobby like his little friend?' the Fat said.

He used his quiet, sly voice which was almost worse than his big voice.

I nodded. 'Give me my mouse.'

'Please?'

'Please, please, please, *please* give me my mouse.'

He smiled, but I couldn't see his eyes behind the blue cigar smoke. 'Of course I'll give it to you, Bobby. But if I do, will you sign that silly paper for me?'

It was awful. I loved the mouse Peter, but I knew that if I signed the paper the name over the store would be changed and it would be just as if Mother and Father and me had never been there at all. Besides, I knew that once the paper was signed the Fat wouldn't have any more use for me and I was afraid for myself.

The mouse Peter's head stuck up from the Fat's big fist underneath his thumb. His thumb had a very sharp, hard looking nail on it. It was like a curved knife.

'Will you sign?'

I shook my head and the thumb slid forward. The mouse Peter squealed and wriggled, but it was held just as if it had been in a mousetrap. It was looking at me when I said: 'No!'

The thumb moved again and the mouse Peter's head went red with blood and then the head came off and the squealing stopped. There was a little sound as the mouse Peter's head hit the floor and then the Fat threw the rest of it down and stamped on it and swore and swore. His face got red and those blue eyes of his came through the cigar-smoke at me, closer and closer until I was lost in them and he was slapping my face and I cried and couldn't stop.

When it was finished he said: 'All right then, you little idiot bastard. This time you're for the boobycoop. You hear me, stupid? The nuthatch!'

The nurse-housekeeper came in afterwards and I was glad of the pills to make me sleepy.

*

The next morning when I woke up I began to plan to run away. I'm not good at planning things usually because I forget what the beginning of the plan was before I come to the end of it, but this time I just had to be clever no matter how hard it was.

The door of my room was locked all the time except when I went to the lavatory or when I went to wash, and then the nurse-housekeeper was always there to watch me. The windows of my room were too high to jump out of or lower myself or anything, so it had to be the lavatory. Actually, I *wanted* to go to the lavatory in the morning, but I held back till after lunch, because I knew the Fat would be at the store and the nurse-housekeeper was always sleepy after lunch. She ate a lot I think.

It was so easy.

All I had to do was put on my jacket and get ready, then when she came in I asked to go to the lavatory. As we passed through the door of my room I pretended to feel funny, then when she wasn't expecting it I pushed her as hard as I could and she fell back into the room. I locked the door then and it was over. She made an awful noise, but she was just as helpless in that room as I had been so I didn't worry about her shouting.

I knew the next thing to do was to get away quickly from the house and the city, but I really had to go to the lavatory first. I was constipated though, so it took quite a long time.

*

I walked and walked as fast as I could till the houses got fewer and there were more trees. I could hear the birds singing and the fresh air was nice after being kept in my room for so long.

Finally I reached a main road right away from the city and the first thing I saw was a sign saying: TO THE WEST. I decided then to go west, to Cornwall, but I didn't know how to do it.

I tried walking, but I was already tired and I knew I'd never walk all the way to Cornwall. I wanted to sit down on the grass at the side of the road and rest, but I was afraid of the Fat, I was afraid he would send policemen to take me back. So I kept going on and on all through the afternoon.

Sometimes people in cars slowed up as they went past me and gave me funny looks, and some of them made signs at me but I didn't know what they meant. Once a car stopped beside me on a bare stretch of the road and the man asked me if I was all right. I said, yes, thank you, and he said are you sure? and I said yes thank you I'm sure and he went away.

I think he thought it was funny that I should be walking along the road all by myself when all the other people were in their cars and lorries, but I don't see what's so funny about somebody walking along a road out in the country. That's what roads are for really. I mean, people were walking along roads long before there were cars or lorries, weren't they?

It was getting cold so I knew night was coming and I began to feel silly having run away so quickly. I hadn't even brought a scarf or anything. It was lonelier too, there weren't so many cars going by on the road and only a few lorries. It was getting dark and I was hungry.

I thought it was a man at first, something tall and shadowy and big by some bushes at the roadside. But it was just a petrol pump, and behind it there were lights, lots of lights and people and music and lorries standing in a row like horses tied up to a rail in a cowboy picture. A sign said: THE JUNCTION CAFÉ. TRANSPORT WELCOME.

I remembered the money then, a half-crown that I'd hidden from the Fat and the nurse-housekeeper. They didn't like me to have any money, though when Mother was alive I always had coins to jingle in my pockets. Nobody looked at me when I went into the café, they didn't *stare* anyway. I went up to the counter and said: 'I'd like a cup of tea please and –'

'Yes?'

It was a girl with a lot of lipstick on, but she was quite nice to me. There was a notice on the wall behind the counter which said: CHEESE ROLLS 9d.

'– and a cheese roll please.'

The tea was sixpence so I had one and three left. I carried my tea to a table without spilling any at all into the saucer, then I went back and got the cheese roll.

It was a good cheese roll with lots of butter, or it might have been margarine, and the tea was sweet and hot. After I'd eaten I just sat there in the warmth and light and held the one and three in my hand inside my jacket pocket. It felt good to have one and three because it meant I could have the same again if I wanted to.

It was interesting in the Junction Café. Most of the people were men with working clothes on, they were driver-men. Some of them read newspapers as they ate and some talked to each other. Some just sat and smoked cigarettes. One of them, a big, dirty looking man with a bald head, was at the table next to mine eating eggs and chips and sausages. I know you're not supposed to stare at people when they're eating, but I couldn't help it. This man wasn't really eating anyway, he was just pushing the food down his throat without looking at his plate at all, and helping it into his mouth with his fingers sometimes. He never took his eyes from a newspaper he had propped against the sauce-bottle, and he made awful noises when he drank his tea.

Then there was another driver-man, a thin, sick looking man. He had a big plate of food in front of him which he hardly touched. He lit a cigarette, but he only smoked a little bit of it before he squashed it out in his food and went to sleep. I don't know how he managed to sleep in all the noise of people talking and lorries coming and going and the music. The music was nice, but I only had one and three so I just waited for other people to put money in the machine and make the records play. I had another cup of tea after a while and that left me ninepence. Then I lost the ninepence in another machine. I had seen a man winning a lot of threepenny bits on it, so I tried after he had finished playing. I pulled the lever as hard as I could, but I lost my ninepence.

After that I just sat and waited and I must have fallen asleep, because the next thing I knew was a man shaking me gently and saying: 'Are yer all right kid?'

Why do people keep asking if you're all right when you're just doing ordinary things like sleeping or walking? I suppose it depends where you are at the time.

I said: 'Yes thank you, I'm all right.'

Then he said: 'Are yer hitching, kid?' He kept calling me kid and he had a funny way of speaking. I didn't know what he meant.

'I mean, are yer tryin' for a lift?' he explained.

A lift! 'Yes please,' I said. 'I'm going to Cornwall.'

'*Cornwall*,' he said, and looked as if he didn't believe me. 'Where's yer gear then?'

I still didn't know what he meant. 'Y'know,' he said, 'yer *gear*. Clothes an' that – yer bag?'

'Oh, I haven't got a bag,' I said.

He looked at me and scratched his head. 'And yer sure yer all right?'

'Yes, thank you, I'm all right.'

'Oh,' he said. 'Well, I'm not goin' to Cornwall, but I'll take yer a bit of the road if yer wait till I have a cuppa tea an' that.'

I said thank you and that I didn't mind waiting. He brought his tea and rolls to my table but he never spoke while he was eating, he just read a paper. Sometimes I caught him looking at me over the paper, but he always just smiled and went on reading. When he was finished eating he lit a cigarette and told me to come on, and we went out to his lorry. It was really dark by this time, so I must have been asleep for quite a while. It said Liverpool on the lorry door, and I knew then that that was why the man spoke so funny. The Beatles come from Liverpool and they spoke like him when I saw them on television. I like the Beatles.

He opened the door for me and helped me up the high step, then he got in at the other side and we drove away from the Junction Café and out along the dark road. I slept again and woke when he shook me as before. We were stopped at a place where the road split into different parts round a grassy island which was lit by high lamps.

'I turn off here, kid,' he said. 'But if yer stand at that corner yer might drop lucky for Cornwall, see?'

He pointed out the place where I had to stand and I got out and waved goodbye as he drove away. He was a nice man, even though he did speak funny. He waved back at me and shouted: 'Look after yerself, kid!' Then he was gone.

I waited at the corner until I got the lorry that took me all through the night to Cornwall. I've already told you what happened to *that* driver-man, so that's all there is to tell about me.

A lepidopterist is a man who kills moths. That's what Mr. Summers told me at breakfast.

He woke me very early, while it was still quite dark, and we had tea and bread and butter and fried eggs. I made the tea and went outside to the lavatory before I ate. It was a wooden place behind the hut with a tin bucket thing instead of a proper bowl and there was no chain. There was a funny sort of flowery smell in there, like disinfectant, but not nice.

I had three eggs and a lot of bread and butter, because Mr. Summers told me to eat up since we wouldn't be back till late that night. He seemed quite excited about something, and I was feeling that way too, though I didn't quite know why. I suppose it was because it was my first day at work. My first day *ever* at work I mean.

Mr. Summers had some whisky after breakfast and smoked a cigarette, and although it was so early I felt more awake than I could ever remember. That was because I hadn't had any pills the night before. I asked Mr. Summers questions about the lepidopterist.

'But what does he do with the dead moths?'

'He sticks pins through them, boy, and keeps them in cases with glass tops. He collects them.'

'Why does he collect them?'

'To look at all the different kinds.'

'Then why does he have to kill them? Can't he look at the different kinds when they're alive?'

'He kills them because he doesn't *think*, boy. He kills them because they are easy to kill.'

'How does he do it, Mr. Summers?'

'You'll see, boy, you'll see tonight. Now let's get ready, we have a long way to go today.'

He let me make more tea, for the thermos flask, and I cut a big pile of sandwiches as well. Cheese sandwiches, my favourite kind. We put the food in our rucksacks with our trowels and cups and things, but we left the sleeping bags on the beds. It was only just getting light when we went out. Mr. Summers locked the door and we went past the bamboo, which was quiet now since there was no wind, and through the gate and out on to the path.

Mr. Summers didn't say very much at first, we just walked on through the quietness until we reached the lanes and after the lanes the road. It was lighter now, but there was mist and the crooked trees still dripped water a little, then all at once there was the sun. The road we were on was a kind of long hill so that we could see a long way. It was magicky again as it had been in the lorry the morning before, and the sun came in streaks across the fields making queer shadows everywhere. The birds were singing in the banks at the roadside and I felt as if something was going to happen.

I don't know what, I just felt that there was something else besides the little trees and the birds and the slow sun. But the light got stronger and everything gradually changed and nothing happened after all. I could see what looked like white mountains very far away. Very neat and white these mountains were, and I asked Mr. Summers about them. He said that they weren't mountains at all, that there were no mountains in Cornwall. He said they were the tips at the place where the china-clay comes from. I was just going to ask about that when he stopped me and took hold of my arm. He pointed along the empty road.

'See them, boy? See them? Aren't they beautiful?'

I looked, but I couldn't see anything and I said so.

'The snails, boy! The snails! Don't you think they look like ships? They carry their shells like great billowing sails, and the antennae look like the prow of some exotic galleon. Don't you think so, boy?'

Mr. Summers was very excited, so I looked again and there they were, just as he said, gliding across the road from one side to the other, like ships a long way off, but so slow. There were lots of them, and although they moved so slowly I could feel that they were in a hurry to get off the road before something happened to them.

'It's always like this in the mornings,' Mr. Summers said. 'They have to complete their mysterious voyages before the birds get too active, and before the cars come.'

'The cars would squash them, wouldn't they?' I said, 'and then we'd have to bury them.'

'Not bury them, boy, I told you before, we just remove what's left and put it where it can't be seen.'

I remembered. 'In the grass or nettles?'

'That's right. Now come on, and step carefully.'

We went on as carefully as we could, and after a long time the sun got very bright and the snails were fewer and fewer until there were none at all. I suppose they all got to wherever they were going.

It was lovely walking in the sun, and Mr. Summers showed me all sorts of things. He showed me primroses and other flowers, and he told me what the different birds were called. Jackdaws and chaffinches and tits and gulls and magpies, but I didn't like the magpies much. They always seemed to be swooping near to have a look at us. It was almost as if they were following us, they were sneaky looking and I didn't like them much at all. But I liked everything else and the time passed very quickly. We must have walked miles and miles before we stopped for tea, because my feet were sore.

We rested for a long time after we'd had the tea and sandwiches and Mr. Summers lay on his back in the grass and smoked. He had found another secret place where no one would disturb us. Mr. Summers knew all the secret places, and to get to this one we had to cross a ploughed field and climb a gate. It was an old house, but so old that it was more grass than stones. There was no roof and only bits of the walls left, and all covered in ivy and grass. It was very quiet there.

After the food and rest I was feeling better, and I took off my shoes and socks to put my feet in the cold grass. That was a good feeling and when I put my shoes and socks on again I felt as if I could have walked a hundred miles. I wanted to get on because I hadn't used my new trowel at all, but Mr. Summers just lay there and kept smoking cigarettes. I wanted to say something but I thought I'd better not since it was my first day at work.

I told you about that didn't I? I mean about it being my *very* first job ever. Most boys go to school and then leave school and go to work. I never even went to school and I never worked at anything at all. But then I'm not really a boy, I'm thirty-one years old. I was never a boy, not like other boys anyway, and I'm not a man like other men. I'm just me.

Then the cow frightened me. It came up to the ruined house so quietly that the first I knew of it was when it snorted right in my ear almost. I jumped up and for a moment I thought I might cry, but it was all right, the cow ran away. I think it was more startled than I was. I sat down again and laughed and Mr. Summers smiled in a wrinkly way without showing any teeth. Mr. Summers never laughed.

'Do you know what that was, boy?' he said.

'It was a cow.'

He shook his head.

'A – a bull?'

'No, no, boy, not a bull.'

'Well, it couldn't have been a calf,' I said, 'because calves are smaller than that.'

'It was life, boy. Life.'

I was getting confused. I wished he'd get up and let us go on so I could try my trowel and do some work, but I had to be polite, so I said: 'Do you mean it was alive?'

'I mean it was *life,* boy. Life in the shape of a cow. Do you understand?'

I didn't, and I had to say so because you're not supposed to tell lies when you're having a conversation with someone. I must have looked as if I was going to cry, because Mr. Summers said not to worry and that he would teach me and there was plenty of time for me to learn.

We left soon after that and I forgot all about it and was feeling fine because we were going to work. We only found one thing that afternoon, a tiny green frog. It was crouched on the road with its arms out as if it was just going to jump, but its legs were crushed, by a car Mr. Summers said. He let me bury it, but it wasn't very much work to bury a little green frog.

*

We walked for hours and hours it seemed, and although I was always looking for things Mr. Summers walked very quickly and hardly paid any attention to the road. The sun was going down by this time and it began to get a bit cold, and dark, it was getting dark. I began to worry a little bit since we were so far from the hut and the sleeping bags, but Mr. Summers kept on till we came to a place where there were some big houses with large gardens and trees and bushes around them.

It was the edge of a village I think, and for a moment I felt a little bit funny about the big houses. They looked quite like the one I lived in before I ran away, but I didn't have time to get sad, Mr. Summers looked very excited and told me to follow him and be as quiet as I could. He crept round the side of one very big house and I followed him over a wall and into some bushes with big, shiny leaves. We lay down there and hid and Mr. Summers said we would stay there until it got darker.

From where we lay there was a view of a lovely green lawn, quite big and smooth, and Mr. Summers stared at it, so I did too. Soon it got to be half-dark and he told me to watch carefully and I would see the lepidopterist. I watched. I'd never seen a lepidopterist before and I was wondering what one would look like. When he did come he was just an ordinary looking man with specs and grey hair, but he was carrying something which made Mr. Summers so excited that he began muttering to himself.

'Deceit! Deceit, boy!' he said.

'What's that he's got?'

'I'll tell you what it is, boy. It's a deceitful machine! It's a light, boy. A light which is so bright that all the moths for a long way come to it, tricked by the brightness you see? You know how a moth will come to an electric light and bang against it till it gets burned or stunned?'

I said yes, I had seen that, and I was going to ask him why they did that but he didn't wait for me to speak. Mr. Summers was very angry.

'That man,' he whispered, 'is a deceiver. He puts out that big light to attract the moths deliberately, then when they come he kills them. We're going to put his light out, boy.'

'How can we do that?'

'Smash it, boy! Smash it!' Mr. Summers' face was twitching and he was breathing funny as well. 'I've been here once before, boy. I smashed it once before.' He felt around him until his fingers closed on a large white stone. 'Now I'll smash the deceitful thing again.'

'Is it part of the work?' I asked.

'Yes.'

'Can I do it, Mr. Summers? Please?'

'Only if you're careful, boy. Well, all right then, I suppose you can run faster than me anyway. Now here's what you do. Take this stone and when the light comes on throw it at the centre of the thing. Throw it *hard*. Smash it!'

'Yes, Mr. Summers.'

'Are you sure you can do it, boy?'

'Yes, Mr. Summers.'

'Right then, he should switch on any time now. When it's done, come back here quickly, pick up your rucksack and follow me. All right, boy?'

I nodded. I couldn't speak any more just then because of the excitement. I felt my feet go as heavy as if they were made of iron and my legs were sweaty and shaking, but I was going to show Mr. Summers that I could do the work no matter what it was. He might like me better then and he might even say he did, he never even called me Bobby, just boy. I didn't mind that, I like being called boy, but it isn't as friendly as Bobby.

'Now!' he whispered.

The light was on. I hadn't noticed it happening but it was on and it was so bright it made the darkness really black around it until my eyes got used to it. I stood up and walked out on the lawn. It was nice and spongy to walk on. Then

I ran, I ran at the light and as I got closer I could hear music coming from the big house. When I was just in front of the light and it was blinding me, I put both hands on the stone and raised it above my head and threw it as hard as I could. There was a loud pop and glass breaking and then it was dark except for the lights which moved in front of my eyes. They weren't real lights though, but the kind I used to get when the nurse-housekeeper gave me too many pills.

The music stopped in the big house and I remembered that I had to run, the trouble was I couldn't remember where in the bushes Mr. Summers was hiding. I ran quickly over the lawn and crashed through the big, shiny leaves looking for him. I heard someone shouting behind me and a dog barking and I was afraid. A hand grabbed my arm and I shouted, but it was only Mr. Summers.

'Hurry boy! Hurry!' He gave me my rucksack and pulled me along to where the wall was and the place where we had come in. We got over quickly, though I kept stumbling because the no-lights were still dancing in my eyes. But we got away. We ran and ran until the noise behind was gone, and then we walked quickly, tripping and stumbling in the dark till Mr. Summers shone a pocket torch and made it easier.

When I had my breath back to where I wanted it I said: 'Did I do it right, Mr. Summers?'

'Yes,' he said, 'you did it *very* right, boy.' Then: 'What's your name, boy?'

'Bobby,' I said. 'I told you already, but you must have forgotten, Mr. Summers.'

'Oh yes, yes. Well, Bobby, you did your job very well. How do you feel?'

'All right but –'

'Yes?'

'Do we have to walk all the way back, Mr. Summers?'

'Perhaps not,' he said, but he didn't sound very sure. Then: 'Very well, Bobby, we'll just walk until we get to a place where we can get a bus to take us somewhere near home. Yes, there's a village about a mile away that'll do quite well. Come on.'

We soon came to the village and it was quite big. Mr. Summers looked at the board at the bus stop which told about the buses and said we had plenty of time. He sounded excited again, but this time he was excited-happy, not excited-afraid or angry. He told me to stay where I was and that he wouldn't be long, then when he came back he had some big bottles of beer and the whisky smell was on him. He gave me two packets of potato crisps though, and they were good because I was hungry after all the excitement. I would have liked a drink, even beer, but I didn't like the smell of it.

*

After that first day's work Mr. Summers nearly always called me Bobby, except when he was angry or when he forgot what my name was because he'd drunk too much whisky, and every day the grass was greener and the flowers were brighter. It was a good time for me. We did our work during the day and at night we went back to the hut to eat and sleep. Once we didn't go back to the hut at all, but slept out in our sleeping bags under the sky. I'd never done that in my whole life. When I woke up in the morning my face was wet, but it was only the dew and I liked it. We had camped out near the sea and I got out of my sleeping bag and walked over the dunes until I came to the last steep sandhill which ran down to the beach.

I was so alone as I walked along that beach that all the other people in the world might have been dead for all I knew. That frightened me a little at first, but then I realized that it wouldn't have made very much difference to me if they had all been dead, except that there wouldn't be any work for me to do. I would have cared if Mr. Summers had been dead though, I liked him.

I thought about the store and Mother and the Fat, and I wished very hard that the Fat was dead. I hated *him*. I knew it was wrong to wish that because Mr. Summers told me never to kill anything, and I didn't want to lose my job. So I stopped thinking about things and filled my pockets with seashells, then I went back to wait for Mr. Summers to wake up so as we could have some breakfast. We had beans in tomato sauce and they're quite good when you eat them cold out of the tin.

*

As the weather got warmer the holiday people started to come to Cornwall and there were cars on the roads all the time. That meant that there was much more work to do. We wandered a very long way from the hut sometimes, sleeping out two or three nights running and buying our food in little village shops. I buried so many things that some of the red paint on my new trowel began to come off, but I still liked the work. We walked mostly in the lanes, away from the cars and people and did our work on the roads at dawn and in the evenings. More and more cars came and the busier the roads got the more whisky Mr. Summers drank, he took to carrying some in his rucksack all the time and drinking it straight from the bottle. He said awful things about the people in the cars, though I thought they looked pretty ordinary, but he was always nice to me. He bought me chocolate and things from the village shops, and a new pair of shoes when my old ones began to break up.

I asked him once about my wages and he said did I really want money? and I said no, not really, but I knew that people got wages when they were working. Mr. Summers said not to worry about it and that if I wanted anything all I had to do was ask.

I waited a while, because I didn't want to be rude, and then I asked for a book about birds and one about the flowers and plants. He got them for me and soon I was learning all the names of the flowers and I could tell the different kinds of birds from quite a long way away.

It was funny, but I was able to read those books quite easily even though I'd always been awful slow at reading and things like that, and another thing, I hardly ever cried at all. Sometimes when we were resting in the middle of the day I used to lie with my face very close to the ground, and I could see all sorts of things among the grass roots that you would never guess were there at all. I used to have dreams as I watched the tiny things in the grass roots, dreams with my eyes open, and sometimes it was as if I were small like the things I was watching. I used to go in there beside them somehow and everything was big around me. I would get *lost* in there, but when I got frightened I always came back to being me again, looking down at the things below my face, so I never cried. All those tiny things seemed to be going somewhere, like the snails in the morning, but I never found out where it was.

I could do what I liked after a while. Once we found a really big gull lying dead at the bottom of a telegraph pole and I didn't bury it right away. I folded the wings and carried it in my arms for hours and hours before I got my trowel out and buried it. Mr. Summers didn't say anything to me about it. He was a nice man.

*

The sunny days were wonderful, though I suppose it all really depended on the mood Mr. Summers was in. He was mostly all right, but sometimes, when he drank too much of the whisky, he got very angry at everything. He was never bad to me or anything like that at all, but when he got angry and sad I used to feel a bit less happy than usual, even if the sun *was* shining.

One day, when we had travelled a very long way from the hut and had slept out in the secret places for two nights running, we were walking along a narrow road when a herd of big brown-and-white cows came towards us in the opposite direction. They filled the whole road and were walking along slow and quiet the way cows do. There was a man with them, a silly looking man with baggy trousers and rubber boots on, he had a stick and was shooing the cows along gently. We stood close to the side of the road to let them get by, and I was very still because Mr. Summers said I might startle the cows if I moved suddenly or anything. They were nearly past us and the man with the stick was saying good-morning and smiling at us, I think he was quite a nice man really but just a bit silly looking, when a car came up from behind the cows and began to toot its horn.

It tooted and tooted and kept on edging forward with its engine growling in a bad-tempered way until it was almost touching the last cow. The man with the stick got all flustered and shouted something at the driver of the car, but the cows were really frightened by this time and began to run and then to gallop. They went in all directions, mooing all the time, their eyes bulging and their heads wobbling like dolls' heads. They were very frightened, but the man in the car just kept on tooting and edging forward until he had scattered the cows all over the place. One of them fell, and I think it hurt itself, because when it got up it was limping, and another one tried to get through a barbed wire fence and cut itself all round its head.

The man with the stick was running all over the place trying to catch them, but he couldn't run very fast in his rubber boots. Finally the driver of the car had a clear path in front of him, but just as he was driving off Mr. Summers ran out and I saw him draw his hand with something in it all along the side of the car. There was a horrible, screeching noise as he did this and when he was finished there was a long, silver scratch on the red paint of the car, right from the front to the back.

The car stopped then and the driver got out. He looked at the scratch as if it was hurting him somehow and ran his finger along it. Then his face got red and he came over to where Mr. Summers was standing with me.

'Did you scratch my car?' he said to Mr. Summers, and he looked frightened as well as angry.

'Yes,' said Mr. Summers, 'but never mind about a little thing like that. You're in a terrible hurry, remember?'

The driver looked back at his red car with the long, silver scratch and from the car to Mr. Summers and from Mr. Summers to me with a puzzled look on his face.

'Is he with you?' the driver said to me, pointing at Mr. Summers.

'No,' I said, '*I'm* with *him*.'

He looked at Mr. Summers in the frightened, puzzled way again. 'I'll have your name and address,' he said suddenly and got out a pencil and a piece of paper.

'I live in a cave underneath the factory at Dagenham,' Mr. Summers said.

I was rude then, I giggled, because I knew Mr. Summers was having a joke, and the man's face got redder. He was bigger than Mr. Summers, but he didn't look strong. He was all clothes, a big coat and a checked cap and string gloves, and he wore specs and had big ears.

'I want that name and address!' the man shouted, but Mr. Summers had drunk an awful lot of whisky that day and he didn't seem to care whether the man was angry or not. He raised his hand in front of the driver's face and waved it about.

'Bless you, my son,' he said. 'In the name of the Rolls, the mini and the holy E-type, I pronounce you a silly –.' He said a word then that I wasn't sure about, but it was a short word that the Fat had called me often and I don't think it's very nice. Anyway, I'm not sure how to spell it.

The man's mouth sort of fell open and I could see he had a lot of fillings in his teeth. He stepped back a little towards his car. 'Is he nuts?' he asked me, pointing to Mr. Summers. I didn't know what to say, but Mr. Summers answered for me.

'Nuts,' he said, 'and bolts. I'm a blasphemer as well. I hate all cars and all motorists, I hold black masses and read the highway code backwards, I make clay models of rally drivers and stick pins in them and when I have to fill up forms I put my religion as pedestrian. Oh, and I slash tyres when I get the chance too.'

He began to walk towards the red car opening his pen-knife as he went. The man swore and kicked Mr. Summers between the legs, then he rushed back to his car and started the engine. Mr. Summers fell down on the road with his face all twisted in pain, holding himself where the driver had kicked him, but as the car drove away Mr. Summers shouted after it: 'Go on, you mini-loving bastard! I hope the arse falls out of your bloody rattletrap!'

*

When Mr. Summers was feeling better he drank the rest of his whisky and took me to a secret place. He said he was going to have a nap and that I could do what I liked but I wasn't to go too far away.

The secret place was among some trees and I was glad, because the shade was nice on such a hot day. I lay for a while beside Mr. Summers and then I saw some flowers that I didn't know. I got up quietly so as not to wake him and went over to have a look at the strange flowers. They were like white bluebells. I went on a little way into the trees and there were more of the white bluebells, lots more. Then I saw a butterfly. I didn't have a book about them yet, so I couldn't tell what kind it was, but it was beautiful and I followed it. I saw more butterflies, all different kinds, and one great big one which wouldn't settle long enough to let me see it properly.

I ran after the big butterfly until I lost it, then I heard somebody laughing. There was some long grass and the laughter came from there, and it was a giggle really, not a laugh. I went down on my hands and knees in the grass and crawled forward towards the sound. After a bit there was a gap and I could see who was giggling. It was a girl and she had a man with her. They were lying close together in the grass and the man must have been tickling her, anyway, her legs were all bare and she was wriggling about and giggling every time he touched her. Sometimes she gave a sort of groan as if he had hurt her, and when he rolled over on top of her she shoved him away. But they were soon close to each other and all the giggling and groaning started again.

It seemed like a silly way to pass the time, I mean just watching people being silly like that, and I was going to crawl away when I saw the big butterfly again. It was a dark, reddish sort of colour with a design on the wings and I wanted to see it up close. It landed on the woman's white jumper and she screamed, but not very loud. At first the man just kept close to her and smiled, but she had stopped giggling and groaning and was whimpering as if she was afraid. She was afraid of the *butterfly*.

The man wriggled against her again and whispered to her, but it was no good, she wasn't playing any more with him. He swore then and picked the butterfly off her jumper. He held it close to her face and laughed, but she only screamed again, louder this time. She stood up and brushed bits of grass and stuff from her clothes, and I heard her saying that she hated the man and wanted to go back to the car. The man got angry when she said that and swore again and squashed the butterfly in his hand. Then he threw it away and stamped on it and *I* got angry.

I stood up from my hiding place and walked over to them. The man had grabbed the woman round the waist and was wriggling against her again, so he didn't see me and I had to tap him on the shoulder.

'Excuse me,' I said, 'but you shouldn't do things like that. It's not right.'

He let the woman go and turned to stare at me.

'It was only a little butterfly,' I said. The woman gave a funny kind of giggle and put her hand over her mouth. Her eyes looked as big as half-crowns. The man just stood there with his mouth open.

'How would you like to be all squashed up like that and

54

killed when you weren't hurting anyone? It's not fair. The butterfly wasn't stopping you playing, he was just –'

The woman started to giggle again, only this time she kept doing it and it was much louder than before. The man's face got red and he tried to hit me, but he missed and tripped himself and that gave me a chance to run away. I could hear the woman laughing and him swearing for quite a long time as I ran, and I'm glad he didn't chase me. He wasn't a very nice man, I think he was a bit silly as well.

*

There was a pub we went to once. It was called THE STRONG MAN, and there was a picture above the door of a man who had no clothes on above his trousers except a funny hat. He was holding a pick in one hand and he looked very strong, with great big muscles everywhere. Mr. Summers said he was supposed to be a miner.

THE STRONG MAN was a cool place inside, cool and half-dark so that I could hardly see after coming in out of the bright sunshine. I was surprised when Mr. Summers took me in with him, he usually told me to wait outside when he went for a drink, but I was glad because we had walked a long way and my feet were sore. There had been more cars on the road than usual, and we'd had a rotten time dodging them on the narrow roads, that was why Mr. Summers took me into the pub I think, so that we could have a drink and a rest. He told me to sit at a table while he went off to fetch the drinks. I had lemonade and he had beer and whisky. He drank his quickly, then he said he was going to have a nap and fell asleep almost at once. I could tell by his breathing that he was asleep.

I sipped my lemonade and kept quiet because I didn't

want to disturb him, and besides, I'd never been in a pub before and I wanted to have a good look at everything. The table we were sitting at was long and shiny and heavy with a bench along the wall behind it. Everything in the pub was heavy and shiny, the beams in the low ceiling, the long wooden bar where you got the drinks and paid, and the man behind the bar. He looked solid and heavy, and the top of his head gleamed where he had a bald place.

There were holiday people there, all talking and drinking in little groups. You could easily tell they were holiday people from the funny way they dressed. There was a woman with orange ski-pants and a blue sweater, and a man with a loose shirt covered with pictures of palm trees. They weren't all holiday people though, there was an old man with freckles on the back of his hands, he had a pipe and a walking stick, and there were two coalmen, I mean the men who deliver the coal. They were black all over, even their faces and necks and hands. Only their eyes and the polished metal studs on their leather back-guards shone bright against the coal dirt. There was a model of a ship as well, a big model of a sailing ship, and as soon as I saw it I wanted to go and have a really close look. I didn't think Mr. Summers would mind if I was very quiet and didn't wake him, so I slid along the bench carefully until I was clear of the table and could stand up. He didn't wake up, in fact he was beginning to snore a little bit.

I went over to the ship where it stood on a shelf in a big glass case, there was a make-believe sea in the case as well, with white wave tops and everything. I was bending over to have a close look when a voice said in my ear: 'Those were the flippin' days, eh?'

I turned my head and there was a face about two inches from the end of my nose. It was a funny sort of face, all pushed out into a very big nose with the chin tucked in so that it could hardly be seen, and the forehead sloping away back to thin, brown hair. The mouth was big and red and wet and the nose itself was like a bent piece of cheese, all greasy and with tiny little holes all over the end of it. But the eyes were the strangest part of the face. They were green, and they stuck so far out that it looked as if they were loose and might roll away down the cheeks at any time. The bottom lids were turned out, red and wet, like a cut under each eye. They were sad eyes.

'Keelhaul and brace the mains'l, eh? Haha.'

As the stranger spoke his breath hit me right in the face, a wind of peppermint with something else under it, something like whisky, but not whisky. I straightened up, because I felt silly with our noses almost touching like that.

'Do you like ships?' he said.

'Yes, I think so.'

He laughed. 'That's right,' he said, 'no harm in a bit of fun, eh?'

He seemed quite a jolly man, a big, not old – not young kind of man wearing a blazer and grey trousers and a shirt the colour of tinned salmon. He held up a glass.

'Not drinking?'

'No.'

'Soon fix that,' he said. 'You on your own?'

I looked over at Mr. Summers. 'Well –'

The stranger put a finger to his greasy nose and winked at me. 'Old boy having a bit of a kip, eh? Never mind, we won't disturb him. Your father is it?'

'No,' I said. 'I mean – he's just –'

He winked again. 'Say no more. Understand and all that. Come and have that drink.'

I went with him to the bar at the far end of the room, well away from Mr. Summers.

'Gin?'

'Lemonade, please,' I said.

The man laughed again, not a loud laugh, but one that moved his whole face, all except his eyes that is, they stayed sad over their red cuts. He put his hand on my arm and gave it a squeeze. 'Lemonade!' he said. 'That's the stuff. No harm in a bit of fun, eh?' He ordered two gins from the heavy, shiny barman.

It was scented and hot going down and I think it made me drunk. The man kept laughing at nothing and talking all the time, but I couldn't understand anything he said because of the gin, except: 'No harm in a bit of fun, eh?' He kept on saying that.

At first being drunk was dreamy and sleepy and happy, then he bought me another gin and the people in the pub began to change. I was a bit afraid then. The two coalmen standing near us changed into beetles after the second gin, the shiny, metal-studded leather on their backs became their shells, and no matter how I turned my head they always seemed to be lying down with the shells uppermost. Their eyes were blinking very slowly as they drank their beer, first their faces would be all black, then the white eyes opened and closed, then the all black faces again. The shells glittered on their backs.

I turned away from them to the barman to see if he was all right, but he was melting. His waxy face was all slipping to one side. I was frightened then, but it was worse when I looked at the woman in the orange ski-pants, because all I could see of her was the pants. Just orange ski-pants with a voice above them. The man with her had palm trees on his shirt and they were waving, waving –

'Sick,' I said.

The man with the sad eyes put his arm round me. 'Sick? Come on, old son, out for a wee-wee.' He laughed. 'No harm in a bit of fun, eh?'

'No,' I heard myself saying, 'no harm in a bit of fun.'

The next thing was a white-tiled lavatory, white tiles with my creamy-coloured vomit sliding down ever so slowly.

'Better?' the man said.

I was feeling better after being sick, much better, but I wanted to pee.

'Can't find the zip?' he said. 'Poor old boy. Here, let daddy. No harm, eh? Got to have a bit of fun sometimes.'

He sounded quite excited. He unzipped me and put his arm round me again and gave me a squeeze like Mother used to, a nice, cuddly squeeze. Then I couldn't find myself, so he put his hand into my trousers to help me, but I peed then and his hand got wet.

'I'm sorry,' I said.

He sighed and got a bit of toilet paper to wipe his hands. 'My boob I suppose,' he said. 'You all right?'

'Yes, thank you.'

He looked so sad, his face as well as his eyes, that I felt sorry for him, but I suddenly remembered Mr. Summers.

'I'd better get back,' I said.

He took my hand. 'You're a nice boy,' he said. 'Maybe we can have another little drink sometime. Sometime when the old boy isn't there, eh?'

'Maybe,' I said. 'Thank you very much.'

That seemed to cheer him up and he came over close to me, so that I thought he was going to kiss me, but just then another man came into the lavatory. The man with sad eyes gave my hand a squeeze and whispered: 'No harm, eh?

No harm in a bit of fun, eh?' Then he was gone. He was a nice, very friendly sort of man, but he had sad eyes.

Mr. Summers was just waking up as I got back. We left THE STRONG MAN and went out into the fresh air which made me feel a bit dizzy.

'Are you all right boy?' Mr. Summers said.

The primroses looked too bright by the side of the road and the trees were waving about a bit, though I couldn't feel any wind on my face.

'I said, are you all right?'

'Yes, Mr. Summers, I'm all right. No harm in a bit of fun eh?'

Mr. Summers looked at me strangely for a while and then told me to stop talking rubbish and hurry up. He never took me into a pub again after that day, but I didn't really mind, we did the work and I was happy. The store and the city seemed very far away, and I had almost forgotten about the Fat.

4: Ice-cream

It was money that caused all the trouble. No, that's not really true, it was ice-cream. One day it was very hot and we had had our rest at dinner time and were walking along a lane close by the sea. All at once the lane opened up and I could see sand and rocks and a lot of holiday people. There was an ice-cream van as well and suddenly I wanted one more than anything. It was so *hot*.

Well, Mr. Summers had said all I had to do was ask if I wanted anything, so I asked for some money for ice-cream. He gave me the money and said he would wait for me up the lane a bit. I knew he didn't like to go on to the sands when there were holiday people there, and especially when there were lots of cars like this time. So I said I would hurry back, because I didn't like leaving him, and I walked up the beach to where the ice-cream van was.

It was yellow ice-cream and very good, but the sun was melting it and it kept dripping off the cone. When I licked it on one side it melted down the other side so I had to lick it pretty fast. I got so busy with the melting ice-cream that for a minute or two I forgot about hurrying back to Mr. Summers as I had said I would. When it was finished I started back, taking a short cut through the cars which were lined up behind the beach, and as I squeezed through between them I saw the bird.

It was a chaffinch and it was dead, stuck to the silvery bit on the front of a little blue car as if it had been glued there as a decoration. I thought about it and realised that the car must have been going fast along the road, and the chaffinch had been darting low down from one bank to the other and the car had hit the bird and the bird had stuck to the car. Dead.

It was sad to think of that little bird going from one place to another and then being killed and carried away by the car and nobody caring. I thought that it was only because it was a bird, and a very little bird, that they hadn't bothered about it. If it had been a person stuck to the front of the car they would have scraped it off and buried it. But not a chaffinch. I took the bird off and was putting it in my pocket when a voice said: 'Bobby? Mr. Robert?'

I let the dead bird drop into my jacket pocket and turned round. There was a man sitting in the next car. He was looking at me and there was a woman with him and she was staring hard as if she couldn't believe what she saw. It was Mr. Whiteside, the floorwalker from the store.

'Is it you, Mr. Robert?' he said. He was getting out of the car.

'Yes,' I said, 'it's me, Mr. Whiteside.'

He was smiling, a real smile, because he liked me and I liked him. I wasn't sure. It was nice to see somebody from the store, but I wanted to get away. I had to get to Mr. Summers again. Mr. Whiteside took my arm. 'Where have you been, Mr. Robert? Everybody's been searching for you all over the place. What have you been doing?'

I was afraid then. I was afraid of them all looking for me. Afraid of the Fat. Even afraid of Mr. Whiteside, who was a nice man.

'Come and have an ice-cream,' he said.

'I've just had one thanks.'

'Oh, come on, Mr. Robert. You can eat another one can't you?'

'I'd better not, Mr. Whiteside. I have to hurry –'

'Is there someone waiting for you, Mr. Robert? Is that why you're in such a hurry?'

I was afraid. I could feel my face going away from me and he must have seen it beginning. He said: 'Oh, come now, Mr. Robert, no tears eh? I'm on holiday. Let's go and have that ice-cream.'

As we walked over to the van I could just see the car out of the corner of my eye. The woman was getting out. I suppose she was Mrs. Whiteside. She smiled at me and I felt a little better, I thought maybe it would be all right. Mr. Whiteside asked me to tell him why I had run away. I did, at least I told him about the pills and how the Fat had hit me. He said: 'Come on now, Mr. Bobby, it's not as bad as that surely?' He said he knew that the Fat wasn't quite the sort of person my Mother had been but that he was all right.

There was something different about Mr. Whiteside. He was still a nice man but I could feel that he was afraid. It was probably the Fat again, he made everybody afraid. I looked back to the car. Mrs. Whiteside had gone. I knew it was all going wrong then and I didn't want any ice-cream, I just wanted to get back to Mr. Summers. I looked around for Mrs. Whiteside as we waited in the ice-cream queue, and I saw her going into the phone-box up the beach where the main car-park was.

It came our turn to buy ice-cream, and as Mr. Whiteside reached up for the cones he let go of my arm and I ran. I didn't pick the direction, I just ran along the sand away from the people and cars as fast as I could. I heard him shouting behind me, but I ducked into some sandhills and ran on. I ran until I came to the lane and on up the lane to where I had left Mr. Summers. But he wasn't there.

It was a different lane. I followed it to the end where it split into two parts and I took the left-hand part because I was sure that would bring me back to where I wanted to be. But it didn't and I started running again. I got lost.

I got lost, lost, *lost*, and I was angry with myself for being so stupid. I came on to the cliff-top in the end and I stopped there to think. I'm not very good at thinking really, but I knew that the best thing to do was find the hut and wait there for Mr. Summers. Our hut lay in one of the breaks in the cliffs, in a little valley near the sea, so all I had to do was find the right valley. But there were so many of them and I wasn't even sure which direction to take. In the end I just guessed the right way and started walking along the cliff-top.

It was hot. There was no one else on the cliff path and the cliffs themselves seemed to stretch away for ever in front of me. I knew that there were breaks in the cliffs though, little valleys and more sandhills and beaches, and I knew that in one of the valleys was our hut. I walked faster. I walked for a very long time until the sun was low in the sky and the heat was less, but I didn't find the hut.

I went down into several valleys and each time the path led me down I felt better, sure that this was the right place, but it never was, and then I would have to start the climb up to the cliffs on the other side again. The paths seemed to get steeper and steeper and each time I felt like crying as I struggled up. I *would* have cried, but I didn't have time. The afternoon was going and I knew it would soon be evening and then night, but I tried not to think about it and instead I watched for flowers and birds that I knew. There were lots of jackdaws and gulls on the cliffs. I wished I could speak to them and ask them the way home. They must have known all the places along the cliffs, and I'm sure if they had known what my job was they would have shown me, but people can't speak to birds.

Just as evening was coming I came to a low wall which ran along beside the path separating a field from the cliffs. I sat on it to rest for a while because my feet were sore, and then I had an idea. I stood up on the highest part of the wall, which was grassy on top, to see if I could see anything from up there that was familiar. I could see inland quite a long way, but although I looked till my eyes were sore I couldn't make out anything special. It all looked familiar and strange at the same time, the lanes are like that.

I nearly fell off the wall with fright when a voice said: 'You lookin' for somethin' special, my handsome?'

It was a farmer-man. I hadn't seen him come up behind me. 'Sort of,' I said, because I had to be careful you see. I got down off the wall and I could feel his eyes on me all the time.

'What sort of thing you lookin' for, my handsome?'

'A place,' I said. I wanted to get away, I didn't like that farmer-man. He was old and bony and all the time he smiled with his mouth and his eyes were bad and not smiling. He had on working clothes, rough trousers held up by braces over a checked shirt, and between the top of his trousers and the checked shirt there were about two inches of his underpants showing, not just the elastic but the rest as well. We had a gardener like that once when Mother was alive and he always had his underpants showing like that. He always smiled like the farmer-man too, with his mouth but not the rest of his face. I didn't like that gardener, he hit me once and laughed at me when I cried and called me bad names.

'A place?' the farmer-man said. 'What place, my handsome?'

I told a lie. 'The place where I work.'

'A farm you mean?' he said.

I nodded.

'I can give 'ee work, my handsome. Pickin' up stones.'

He came closer and it was as if his eyes were inside my pockets and everything. He had a wart on his nose with hairs coming out of it and his eyes were yellow where they should have been white. 'Do 'ee fancy it, my handsome?'

'I beg your pardon?' I said.

'Do 'ee fancy pickin' up stones?'

'Stones?'

'Four bob an hour – four an' six,' he said. 'Fancy it, my handsome?'

He took hold of my arm with fingers as big as bananas and as hard as wood and he pulled me over to a gate in the wall. He waved a hand at the field. 'There they be, my handsome. Stones.'

On the dark ground the stones were spread out white and jagged over the field. I didn't want to pick up stones, I wanted to find Mr. Summers, but I couldn't help wondering why the stones had to be picked up and how. It didn't seem a very good job to me.

'How do you do it?' I asked him.

' 'Tis easy, my handsome. You just picks 'em up and piles 'em an' then I comes along with the tractor an' we loads 'em up an' dumps 'em. See?'

'Why?' I said.

He looked at me for a long time, his mouth smiling even wider than before but his eyes were cold and shifting all the time. 'You say you works on a farm, my handsome?'

'Not all the time,' I lied. Then I remembered the dead chaffinch in my pocket. I took it out and showed him. 'This is my job really.'

He forgot to keep his mouth smiling when he saw the bird. He took it out of my fingers and turned it over in his hands, then he began to laugh, and the laugh made him even nastier than before.

'My Christ!' he said, 'you call this your work? 'Tis rubbish. Just rubbish!' He threw the bird out over the edge of the cliff and pointed to the stones in his field. 'I spend *years* pickin' them stones up. Years! And all you do is fart about with dead birds.' He was angry but still laughing.

'You know what you are, my handsome?' He came so close to me that I could smell him. 'You're a looney, my handsome. A *looney*! HAHAHAHAHAHA –'

He pushed his face forward so that I had to bend over backwards to stop his nose touching mine and his laughter was going right up my nose and into my mouth as well as my ears. It was beating round my head and bouncing off my eyes. I began to cry and he laughed louder. That made me angry, so I kicked him, on the knee I think. Then I turned and ran as fast as I could along the path away from the field with the stones and the farmer-man with his underpants showing. He chased me for a while but he was old and I soon left him behind. I'm quite good at running.

I found some more valleys that night, but not many and not the one I was looking for. I was tired and hungry and my feet were sore. I thought of having supper in the hut, and about my nice warm sleeping bag which was still on the bed where I had left it in the morning and I cried, but the crying didn't help at all. It was quite dark suddenly and getting darker, so I lay down at the foot of a grassy wall near the path and tried to sleep. It took me a long time to get to sleep because I was cold and unhappy, and even when I did drop off the cold made me wake up again. It was an awful long time till morning.

*

I was walking again as soon as it was light enough to see my way. I was stiff and freezing and I wanted a nice cup of tea more than anything, more than food even, and I was *really* hungry. After a while the path dropped down again, but this time I didn't rush down into the valley, I stood and looked and I could see it wasn't our valley. The path up the other side looked so long and steep that I didn't want to have to climb up it. I couldn't, I was too tired. So I turned inland and went over a gate and through a field and then another until I came to a lane. I felt a bit better then, I thought that if I followed the lane maybe I would find Mr. Summers, and it would be easier walking anyway.

But the lane twisted and turned and I didn't know which way I was going. I was afraid then, afraid that I might never find the valley and Mr. Summers, and I did a stupid thing. I began to run, and when I came to another lane I rushed off up there. I kept doing this, and I think I was crying all the time, until my legs were so tired I could hardly stand up, let alone run, but I *did* keep running. It was being afraid that made me run like that, and I wasn't going much faster than when I walked. I ran right up to a farm gate and two big dogs barked at me and tried to get over the gate. I heard a woman's voice but I didn't stop to see who it was, I just ran until I couldn't run any more. Then I was on my knees in a lane, trying to get my breath to do what I wanted to do, when the cows came.

They were coming fast down the lane towards me, running and mooing and I could hear a man shouting behind them. They were big cows, they filled the lane from bank to bank and they were brown and black and white with sharp looking horns and stamping feet and I shouted to them to stop, but they weren't going to so I had to get up and run again.

I got away from the cows and came out on to a road. I walked close to the edge of the road while the cars went by, and I felt so bad that I almost wished one of the cars would stop and the driver ask me, are you all right? But nobody bothered with me, they had all kept noticing me when I didn't need them, but now that I was all wrong nobody looked at me at all.

I knew what was wrong. I was lost. So I turned off the road up a lane, because I didn't like being on a busy road and I might as well be lost up a lane, at least there were flowers there. I looked in my rucksack to see if there was maybe something to eat that I had forgotten, but there wasn't. Then I passed another farm where there was a man leaning on a gate and I thought I'd ask him which way the sea was. He was a fat man, not as fat as *the* Fat, but fat, and he was eating crisps. He had a red face, a frightened kind of face like the cows that had chased me, and he wore a brown overall coat and a cloth cap. He had rubber boots all covered in mud and hairs coming out of his nose in bunches.

'Good morning,' I said, and he nodded.

'Which is the way to the sea please?'

His eyes bulged like the cows' eyes when I said that, but he didn't speak, he just pointed.

'That way?' I said.

He nodded, munching the crisps as if he was starving. *I* was starving and I didn't have any crisps. I would have asked him for one, but I don't think he would have liked that. One crisp isn't much anyway. I thanked him and went on, and he was right. I could smell the sea.

I hurried on until I felt the ground sloping down and I wished as hard as I could that it would lead to our hut. It began to look familiar around me, but I wasn't sure until I heard the sound. It was bamboo!

Soon there was the path and the gate and the bamboo itself and I was home. Mr. Summers wasn't there, so I sat on the step to wait for him. I wasn't going anywhere.

The next thing I remember is waking up inside my sleeping bag. I lay still in the warm with my eyes shut and then it all came back to me, right up to the time when I had sat on the step. I opened my eyes and tried to sit up, but something pushed me gently down again. It was Mr. Summers.

'Lie still, Bobby,' he said. 'You lie still and I'll make you some nice tea. Would you like that?'

I was so happy to see him again that I couldn't speak in case I might cry. I cry sometimes when I'm very happy or excited as well as when I'm afraid or mixed up. I just nodded and he went away to get the tea.

I lay looking up at the roof of the hut and tried to remember what had happened, but all I could get up to was sitting on the step. I could remember about the ice-cream and Mr. Whiteside, and I could remember the underpanted man and the cows chasing me and the silly man with the potato crisps. After that the sound of the bamboo and the step I had sat on. Then nothing.

I would have to tell Mr. Summers about Mr. Whiteside and his wife going to phone and everything. I would have to tell him about the Fat and Mother and the store. I would have to tell him something else as well, and then he might not let me work with him any more. But I would *have* to tell him.

You see, I knew why I couldn't remember anything between the time I sat on the step and waking up. I had been ill. I'd had one of my fits. I don't know why people call them fits. That's a word that makes you think of neat things joining together, everything in its place. It's not like that at all.

It's red and noisy at first and then black and silent and lost. It leaves an empty bit that you've forgotten all about. A bit that doesn't fit anywhere.

Mr. Summers came back with a cup of tea. 'You drink that, Bobby, while it's nice and hot.'

'I've got something to tell you, Mr. Summers,' I said.

'After you've drunk the tea, then you can tell me. Are you hungry?'

I was starving and I said so. He went off again and while he was away I drank the tea and it was good. Mr. Summers brought some more tea and some beans on toast, which was my favourite, and bread and butter and cheese and choco-late biscuits and an apple. It was so wonderful that I forgot all about telling him everything until I had eaten every single thing and drunk all the tea. Then I felt so much better that I began to wish I hadn't said anything about telling. I just wanted everything to stay the way it was. But I had to tell.

He sat and smoked one cigarette after another while I told him about what had happened the day before. I told him all that, and then I went right to the beginning and told him all about the store and Mother and the Fat. Last of all I told him about my fits. I said they didn't happen often, especially when I was happy, but I said that they *did* happen. Then I asked him if I had to go away.

'No, you don't have to go away, Bobby.'

'And I can keep on with the work?'

'Yes.'

'And I can live here with you, Mr. Summers?'

'Yes.'

He had the wrinkly smile on his face and I could see his eyes. That didn't happen very often, and they were such pale eyes that it took a long time to find out what was in them when you did get a look at them. I could see what was in Mr. Summers' eyes now and it was good.

I said: 'Mr. Summers?'

'Yes, Bobby?'

'I love you, Mr. Summers.'

He didn't say anything, he just looked at me without smiling for a while and then got up and fetched the whisky and a glass. 'Bobby?' he said.

'Yes?'

'Bobby, was that all true about the – the Fat, and everything? About the store, the mouse, everything?'

'Yes, Mr. Summers, it's all true. And now they know I'm down in this part of the country they'll come looking for me. So it might be better – better for you I mean – if I went away. But I don't want to. I want to stay.'

'You will stay, Bobby, you will stay. But we won't go out for a while in case they are looking for you. Besides, you're still not well, boy. Try to go to sleep now, that'll make you better.'

As I closed my eyes I heard the clink of the whisky bottle against the glass.

*

I had dreams. I had nightmares.

The good dreams I can only half remember, but the other things are still there today, like pictures that you sometimes see and can't ever forget.

I didn't know whether it was night or day, or really whether I was awake or asleep sometimes. In the dark there were the mouse-noises, and sometimes I knew it was the mice. Other times it sounded more like fingers scraping at the hut to get in. The Fat's fingers. More than five on each hand, white and fat and strong and cruel with the rings flashing like eyes.

It was always the same. In the nightmare I would be going along a lane all by myself, a horrible lane with black grass on the banks and black flowers on the bushes, and the spiky leaves of the bushes were real spikes like needles. I hurried along the lane, knowing that there was something I had to do, something very important. Then I would see something lying there, a bird or a hedgehog or a crushed snail, and I would hurry to it with my trowel. But when I reached it it wasn't a dead animal waiting to be buried, it was a hand with lots of fingers and rings which had eyes in them. Hard, blue eyes like the Fat's eyes.

They *were* the Fat's eyes, and it *was* the Fat's hand.

I beat it with my trowel until it stopped wriggling, and then I tried to dig a deep hole to bury it, but the ground was like stone and I couldn't even scratch it. The hand began to wriggle again, and then it *crawled*. Like a big, white, hairy spider with lots of blue eyes.

I would run then and run and run until I came to the bamboo, but the bamboo was changed into a jungle of waving stems and I had to force my way through. All the time I could hear the hand scrabbling behind me and I was crying and calling for Mr. Summers. But Mr. Summers never came.

Then suddenly I was through the bamboo and in the garden, racing for the door. I just made it and slammed the door shut on the hand, then I ran to the bed and jumped into my sleeping bag. I pulled it up over my head and stuck my fingers in my ears to shut out the noise of the hand as it scraped and scraped to get in.

And it always finished the same way. I would feel something pulling at the sleeping bag around my face and I would think it was the Fat's hand. Then I would scream and scream until Mr. Summers' voice came through it all and I'd wake up. Mr. Summers was always nice to me then. He would give me nice things to eat and sit and talk with me about the birds and flowers and the little animals. Then there came a time when it all stopped. I remember waking up covered in sweat, with the sunlight streaming through the windows looking very clean and warm. I lay listening to the bamboo moving in the wind and the gulls crying and the sea-sound, and I knew I was better.

Mr. Summers came with tea and sat by the bed to talk with me.

'I'm going to tell you a story, Bobby, and I want you to listen carefully.' He fetched the whisky and poured himself a big glass.

'First of all, Bobby, there was a man who worked in a bank. He worked hard until he became manager of the bank, but it took him a very long time. Then he got married and bought a lovely house on the edge of the town. It was a big house with a huge garden. He didn't really want such a big place, but the woman he married did. She wanted every-thing, everything except love, Bobby. She wanted clothes and money and a fine house and friends who had these things. The man kept going to the bank and he worked very hard, but when he came home at night the woman would fight with him and tell him he wasn't working hard enough, or they could have had a better, bigger house. The man became very unhappy, and the thing which made him most unhappy was that there was no love in the big house.'

Mr. Summers took another long drink of whisky and lit a cigarette. 'Then there was the garden,' he went on. 'There was this huge garden. The woman spent a lot of his money on the garden. There was a fishpond and trelliswork and a hothouse, there were lawns and even a palm tree. She made the man work in the garden, although she knew he hated it. He hated gardens! This man liked wild things and she made him tear out the wild flowers and plant tame shop plants. It was a poisoned place that garden. The woman bought things and made the man sprinkle them and spray them, and they were bad things which killed. She made the man kill all the time. She made him kill mice and butterflies and snails and caterpillars, and she made him take the life from intricate little insects. You see, the woman thought the garden was a place to be made neat and ordered like a room in a house.'

Mr. Summers took more whisky. 'And the man had a dog, Bobby, a dog called Toby. Just a little dog, a quiet, friendly, little dog. The woman gave the dog some of the poisoned stuff one day and killed it. Oh, she said it was an accident, but the man *knew*. The man got tired, his life was the bank and the house and the garden, and he became very tired and unhappy.'

'But why did the man let the woman poison everything? Why didn't he stop her, Mr. Summers?' I asked. Mr. Summers had the wrinkly smile on his face, but he looked very sad.

'Well, I don't know if you can understand, but you see, the man was a good bit older than the woman, and in a way which I don't think you'll know about, he was afraid of her. Some people just kill, Bobby, and she was one of those people. Oh, I don't mean that she was really bad, but some people just have to kill, they don't think about it, it's just a part of them. Perhaps they secretly want to die themselves, I don't know about that. Things started to get worse for the man, he made bad mistakes at his work and he felt ill all the time. He began to drink whisky, but that only helped for a little while and soon nothing helped him. He felt as if his life was one long, dark, wet afternoon and he wanted to die. But he couldn't die, he was too afraid of the woman even to kill himself, besides, he knew that if he did kill himself it would really be the woman killing again in a roundabout way. So, he killed the woman.'

'How did he kill her, Mr. Summers?'

'With the poison Bobby. He killed her with the poison and then he burned her body in the garden incinerator, a big, brick incinerator which she had had specially built to take the garden rubbish. Then the man ran away from the house and the garden and the bank. He ran away and nobody ever caught him for killing the woman. That was just and right, Bobby, because killing her had been a good thing.'

He had finished his story. He sat back and lit another cigarette, and I thought about what he had told me. I understood it all, but I couldn't see why he had told me the story in the first place. He was watching my face. Then he said: 'I was that man, Bobby.'

'But you don't kill things!' I shouted.

'I did that time. That one time, Bobby, because it had to be done. I did it secretly and quietly and then I took a great deal of money from the bank. I wandered for a time, all over the country, until I came here. The place was for sale, for *cash* sale and no formalities. I own it under a false name. Wait, I'll show you something.'

He got up and went to the cupboard where he kept the food, and at first I thought he was trying to push it over, but he only moved it a bit. There was a loose plank in the floor where the cupboard usually stood, he prized it up with his penknife and lifted something out from underneath it. It was a metal box, black, with a lock on it. He carried it over and laid it on the bed. He got his keyring out and when he had found the right key and opened it I saw more money in there than I had ever seen all at once. Even more than I used to see at the store sometimes when Mother took me. It was like a big sandwich box, only instead of sandwiches there were bundles of notes, five pound notes, all packed in tight.

'There are two more boxes like this one Bobby. All the money I, or we, can ever use. Especially the way we live here.'

I was glad he had all that money, I knew money was important.

'So we can stay here for ever?' I asked him.

He nodded. 'Or some other place like this. But there is one thing to do before we can settle, and that is to make you better.'

'But I *am* better, Mr. Summers, honestly.'

He shook his head. 'You won't be all right till we take away the thing that gives you such terrible dreams. We have to remove something, Bobby.'

I was scared then. I was scared of having things removed. They took me away to have my tonsils removed once and it was horrible. I'd been to the dentist as well and I was scared.

'What is it, Mr. Summers? Is it something inside my head?'

'No, Bobby. It's the Fat. We have to kill the Fat.'

It felt as if the bed had risen off the floor and was floating, swaying gently from side to side. All the usual buzzing noises which are always working away somewhere inside my head suddenly stopped, and it was so quiet floating there in my sleeping bag that I thought the world had stopped moving, and all the stars and the sun and the moon as well.

'Then you'll be free, Bobby.'

The bed hit the floor with a thump and everything was

back to normal again and I knew he was right! I laughed.

'Yes, oh, yes!' I shouted. 'We'll have to kill the Fat! To kill the Fat! To kill the FAT!'

Mr. Summers had to give me a good shaking in case I had one of my stupid fits. We had some food then, and I got up later and had a walk round the garden. My legs were shaking a lot, maybe because I'd been in bed so long, or maybe because of the excitement. I stamped my feet on the ground and wished the muscles in my legs to get strong again. I wished I was strong in all my muscles, I wished I was big, and tall, and *strong*. Strong enough to kill the Fat.

Mr. Summers gave me a little of his whisky after supper to make me sleep he said. He was right, I slept well and didn't dream at all.

6: To Kill The Fat

We began by walking. Out of the hut and up the path into the lane. From the lane to the road, and from the road to a village. We got a bus there, an old, smelly, country bus which took us to town. Then there was the railway station and the train. The train was exciting for me because I'd never been on one before, when Mother took me anywhere it was always in a car with a special man to drive it and open the door and everything. She always said that trains might get me too excited.

Going on the train with Mr. Summers got me excited all right, but not too much. While we were waiting for the train to go I went to have a look at the engine, but it wasn't like the ones I had seen pictures of in books. There was no steam at all, and it was a different shape as well, squarish and big. But it quivered all the time and looked strong and I was sure it would get us there all right even without steam. We had tea while we were waiting and Mr. Summers bought rolls and fruit pies in packets, then he took me to the book-stall and I got a lot of comics to read on the way.

For a long time we had a carriage to ourselves on the train, long enough for me to read all my comics, then we had to get out and take a different train. The second train was much busier than the first one, and there were men with umbrellas and leather briefcases in our carriage, so I knew we must be getting near the city. I must have slept for a while, and when I woke up we were there. In the city. In my city.

We ate again in the railway station, a proper dinner with potatoes and everything, and then we went out into the street. It was getting dark and the shops were all closed, but Mr. Summers went into a pub and bought a little, flat bottle of whisky.

I was glad it was dark, because no one could really see who I was. We walked out of the city towards the part where I lived, and on the way I pointed out all the places I knew to Mr. Summers, but he wasn't very interested. I know he didn't like the cities, and besides, he was afraid. So was I. I was afraid of the Fat. I was afraid of him and we were going to kill him. Suddenly I realised that I didn't know how to kill anybody.

'How do we do it, Mr. Summers?'

'Do what, boy?' I knew he was afraid then, because he forgot to call me Bobby.

'I mean how do we kill him?' I said.

'I have a knife,' Mr. Summers said. He pulled it from his pocket quickly to let me see and put it back again, then he had a drink from the flat bottle. It wasn't a very big knife, and it didn't look very sharp either. I was sure it wasn't big enough to go into the Fat, not right *into* him to get to where he was under all the fat and kill him. But then I thought how clever Mr. Summers was, he'd find a way to do it, and anyway, I was there to help him.

As we got close to the house I began to recognize trees and bushes and other houses. Once I saw a dog I knew quite well, I spoke to it, but the dog didn't come to be petted, it just looked at us in a frightened kind of way and ran off. It must have known what we were going to do. That made me feel lonely, and as it got darker it got colder. I began to shiver a bit.

Then we were at the house, my house. There was only one window with a light. I knew a secret way in through the hedge and across the lawn at the back, and we crept up till we could see in the lighted window, which was on the ground floor at the side. There were some people there I had never seen before. One was a cook I think, because he had white clothes on, he was with a woman in a black dress. There was another man with a car-driver's uniform on and a young girl dressed as a maid. The nurse-housekeeper wasn't there though, the Fat must have sent her away. He would have been very angry when he knew I had escaped.

They were all strangers. The cook had the woman in black sitting on his lap and the car-driver was dancing with the maid. There was music and they were laughing and looked happy. That was bad, because I knew nobody could be happy in a house where the Fat was.

'He's not here, Mr. Summers,' I whispered.

'He *must* be here boy,' he whispered back. 'He *must* be here. Maybe he's asleep.'

'No. He's not here, Mr. Summers. I just know.'

We went away from the window, and at first I felt glad that the Fat wasn't there, then I felt afraid. I sat on the swing on the lawn for a minute to think. It was a good swing, you could go as high as you liked and it never squealed or shook. I swung gently while Mr. Summers pushed me and then I knew what we had to do.

'We have to go to the store, Mr. Summers.'

'The store?'

'I think that's where he is. He'll be at the store working in his office. He did that sometimes when I was here.'

'Do you know the way, Bobby?'

'Oh, yes. I know, Mr. Summers.'

Mr. Summers took a long drink of whisky and threw the bottle away. 'Then we must go to the store, Bobby. You lead the way and I'll follow.'

I'd never led anybody anywhere before so I had to be

careful. It was very late by this time and the street lamps were on. As we came to the last turning before the street where the store was I was wishing hard. I was wishing that my name would still be there in big letters above the main door. It was, all lit up by a street-lamp and I was glad. But there was something else as well. The Fat's car. It was foreign I think, and big and black and silver and unfriendly looking. It was too big for an ordinary person really, so it could only have been the Fat's car. I was scared then, because the Fat was somewhere in the store, which was all dark and closed. We had to go in and kill him.

Mr. Summers touched my arm and pointed up. I looked, up to the third floor where there was a light in one window.

'Would that be his office, Bobby?'

I nodded. 'I think so, Mr. Summers. Mr. Summers?'

'Yes?'

'I have to go to the lavatory quickly. I'm sorry.'

There was a public one not far away and Mr. Summers took me there and gave me a penny. Afterwards I felt better, but not much.

We had to find a way to get in, but the doors were all locked, even at the back, and I was getting more and more afraid all the time. I wished that we could go back to the station and go home again, but Mr. Summers said no, we had to go on with what we had come to do. We got in through a window at the back. Mr. Summers opened it with his knife and we climbed in one after the other, him first and then me. It was a very small window, so it was a good job we were both little people.

I fell in on the other side on top of Mr. Summers and he swore. We were in a lavatory and one of my shoes got soaking wet because I put my foot in the bowl as we fell. Mr. Summers was whispering: 'We have to be very quiet now,

Bobby. Do you know the store well? Even in the dark I mean?'

I said yes, I thought so, because I'd been there so many times. He told me to lead the way again – to the Fat's office this time. Mr. Summers closed the window carefully and we went out into the store, out into the dark. I knew there was a watchman, an old man with a big black rubber torch. I told Mr. Summers about him, and he said it would be all right if we were very quiet.

The store wasn't like it was in the daytime at all. It was so quiet and dark and nearly everything was covered with white sheets. We went through the part of the ground floor where all the ladies' things are, handbags and brooches and gloves and everything, until we came to the main staircase. It was very dark there, and I didn't like it at all. I wanted to try to see if the lifts were working, but Mr. Summers wouldn't let me, he said it would make too much noise. So we climbed the stairs, our feet quiet on the carpeting, until we reached the first floor. I would have liked to have stopped there for a while to see what sorts of pets the pet department had, but Mr. Summers made me go on. There was the second floor with furniture and carpets and things like that, and then the last climb to the third floor.

The clothes were there, men's and women's clothes in different parts separated by the shoe department. The Fat's office was over on the other side. My eyes were accustomed to the darkness now, but I don't know if that was good or bad. It meant that I could see where I was going better, but I could half-see some things as well and that wasn't very nice. There were lots of dummies, the ones which wear the suits and dresses, and they stared at me. I used to think they had nice faces, but that was in the daytime, now they were like the people we had seen through the window at home.

Strangers, frightening in the dark and silence. Mr. Summers was behind me though, and that made me brave. He had the knife.

We made our way past the dummies and the counters all covered in their white sheets. I was leading Mr. Summers to the door which opened on to a corridor where all the offices were. The Fat's office was at the end of the corridor.

It was easy to find the door, the light from inside the office spilled out underneath it, but when I did reach it I couldn't open it. I just couldn't, my hands and fingers weren't working properly. Mr. Summers opened it, very softly and carefully, and we were in the half-dark corridor. He closed it again without the slightest sound and laid his fingers to his lips to tell me to be quiet. I nodded, I couldn't speak anyway, my throat was all closed up with the fear. It was a long walk to the end of the corridor where the grey-glass of the Fat's door was, and when we got there we just stood there waiting for something. It was the fear, it had stopped us. Mr. Summers was clutching the knife in his pocket, but he wasn't doing anything else. I made it happen. I knocked on the Fat's door.

There was no answer right away, then the Fat's big, heavy voice said: 'Come in.'

*

We went in, me first, and as soon as I had opened the door there was the Fat's smell. It was the smell of the big, brown cigars that he smoked mixed with his own smell, he sweated a lot you see.

He was behind the big desk that used to belong to Mother. His eyes jumped across to mine and I was frozen in the open doorway, they were bluer than ever those eyes and I could see right into the Fat. I would have turned and run away, but I wasn't able to move.

'Come in, Bobby,' the Fat said.

I moved then and Mr. Summers came in behind me and closed the door. The Fat was surprised, he looked quickly from me to Mr. Summers and back again. I watched carefully to see if there was any fear in the blue eyes, but there wasn't. Nobody frightened the Fat.

'Well, well, Bobby, and where have you been hiding yourself, eh?'

He switched to Mr. Summers. 'I don't believe I know this gentleman. Introduce us, Bobby, don't forget your manners.'

'This is Mr. Summers,' I said.

The Fat watched Mr. Summers for a while, then he pushed his big face about until it looked as if it was smiling. He took a bottle out of his desk and two glasses.

'Will you have a drink, Mr. Summers? I don't know how to thank you for bringing my Bobby back to me.'

'I didn't bring him back,' said Mr. Summers.

'And I'm not *your* Bobby,' I said.

The Fat made his face look surprised, but it wasn't real, nothing the Fat's face did was real. 'Oh? Well, the main thing is that you are back, Bobby. Now, let's have that drink, Mr. Summers. I take it there is something you want to see me about?' Mr. Summers watched as the drinks were poured out. I knew he must be wanting one badly, but he didn't move to take the glass the Fat offered him.

'I've come to kill you,' Mr. Summers said.

The Fat drank the whisky he'd been going to give to Mr. Summers and then picked up his own glass. He put a new cigar in his mouth and lit it with his big silver lighter.

'I see,' he said. 'Why?'

'Because you're an evil man.'

The Fat drank off his whisky and filled both glasses again. 'You're sure you won't have a drink, Mr. Summers. It's the best I assure you, the very best.'

I could see how hard it was for Mr. Summers to refuse the drink. So could the Fat. He held the glass out to me.

'Here you are, Bobby, give this to Mr. Summers.'

I don't know why I reached out for the whisky, I suppose it was because I'm so stupid. Perhaps I thought that if Mr. Summers had some whisky he would feel better and braver and he might kill the Fat quickly and we could go home. Anyway, I reached out for the glass and the Fat dropped it and grabbed my wrist. He twisted my arm behind me so that I was lying across the desk on my back. He was hurting me.

'Now,' said the Fat, 'let's have whatever it is you've got in that pocket, Mr. Summers. Move!'

My arm was being twisted harder and harder and I began to cry. I couldn't help it, but I kept shaking my head at Mr. Summers to tell him not to give the knife to the Fat. Then the Fat brought his cigar down over my face, so close to my skin that it was burning me without quite touching me.

'Well?' he said to Mr. Summers.

Mr. Summers took out the knife. 'On the table,' the Fat said. When Mr. Summers laid the knife on the table the Fat took his cigar away from my face, but he still held my arm and hurt me.

'Now *sit*, Mr. Summers,' he said. Mr. Summers let himself down into a chair and the Fat picked up the knife and put it in his pocket. Then he sort of threw me away, and when I looked up from the carpet he was standing by the door and laughing.

I realized then how small we were. Mr. Summers and I, compared with the Fat. It was all going wrong, and although I knew something awful was going to happen all I could do was lie on the carpet and cry. His laughter was terrible. It filled the room and my head till I thought it would burst. Then he said: 'Don't lie there blubbering, you idiot. Get up and sit in the other chair. *Get up*!' I was so scared that I did what he said without even knowing it. I knew when I was sitting in the chair but I couldn't feel it under me, I couldn't feel anything except being afraid.

'Where have you been all this time, you booby? And who is this little runt you've brought with you? *Tell* me.'

'I've been in Cornwall,' I said. 'Working for Mr. Summers.'

'Working? You? What the hell could you work at, you half-witted bastard?'

'I was working with the little animals,' I said. 'Please let us go. I won't come back again. You can have the store and everything. Please –'

He laughed again and it was like a gust of bad wind.

'You know,' he said, 'I'd keep you for kicks if you weren't such a little drip. And for your information, my Bobby booby, the store isn't yours to give. It's *mine* now.'

'But my name,' I said. 'My name is still above the door –'

'Goodwill, booby, goodwill. But you're too thick to understand that. The – store – is – mine, get that through your puffy little skull and don't try to bargain with me.'

Mr. Summers had been sitting with his face in his hands, but now he looked up and said: 'What are you going to do?'

The Fat rocked back on his heels and blew out a little cloud of cigar smoke. 'Well, *Mr.* Summers, I could lift that phone and get the police for you, and I could put the nitwit in the looneybin where he deserves to be and that, as they say, would be that. But – I'm not too keen on the police and I don't want the bother of getting that fool put away. These things are bad for business, they get around. Most people have forgotten about our Bobby and I want it to stay that way. I'm an opportunist, *Mr*. Summers, and you've given me an opportunity, it's as simple as that. Simple enough for the booby to understand – almost.'

He laughed again. 'I know roughly where you've been, Bobby booby. Remember the meeting with Mr. Whiteside?'

I had forgotten the phone call that Mr. Whiteside's wife had made, and now the thought of the Fat finding our valley and the hut came. It was like the nightmare come true, he *was* going to find the hut and there was nothing I could do about it. But maybe Mr. Summers –

'It won't take us long to get down there in the car,' the Fat said. 'Nice and quiet down in Cornwall. Out of the way, you know? Oh, there is one little thing before we go. I know you'll do what you're told, Bobby booby, but your friend here –'

He rumbled over to where Mr. Summers sat with his face in his hands, looking smaller than ever in the great big chair. The leather armchairs were soft and comfortable, but they were far too big for Mr. Summers and me and we were lost in them, our feet hardly touching the ground.

'Stand up, *Mr*. Summers,' the Fat said.

Mr. Summers sat where he was. 'If you hurt that boy I'll –'

The Fat laughed. 'You'll what, *Mr*. Summers?'

He grabbed Mr. Summers then as if he was just an old coat or something and began punching him hard in the body. His big fist with the rings went in and out, in and out, but Mr. Summers only made a noise at the first punch. After that his face went white and there was only the sound of punching.

I felt sick. I opened the door quietly and went out without the Fat seeing me. I didn't vomit or anything, I just felt dizzy and hurt inside as if it had been me getting punched and not Mr. Summers. I passed the dummies and went down to the first floor where the pet department was. They were all sleeping in their cages. The little birds and the puppies and the tortoises and everything. I had a look at them all and then I wandered about till I came to the sports department. There was a bit of light on the first floor from the high lamps in the street outside and I could see a patch of what looked like grass, though it was only a kind of paper really, and there was a tent on the grass, a real tent with beds and everything inside. I went into the tent and lay down on the bed and hid. I thought maybe if I lay very still the Fat wouldn't find me.

As I lay there the sick feeling went away and my head became clearer inside, clearer than I could ever remember. I could see my stupid self lying there, not a boy and not a man and thirty-one years old, and I got angry. Mostly with myself for being so stupid, but angry with the Fat as well for being so bad. I could have stayed there, hidden in the tent on the paper grass that the window-dresser had made. Oh, yes, I could even have run away, but I saw clearly now why Mr. Summers had wanted to kill the Fat and I was ashamed to be hiding.

I got out of the tent and looked around the sports department until I found what I wanted. A sheath-knife, much bigger and stronger than the silly little thing Mr. Summers had brought, and much sharper too. I went back then. Up the stairs and up and up, and past the dummies again until

I came to the corridor. Down the corridor and through the door, and there he was. The Fat.

He was behind the desk again, sitting with whisky in one hand and a cigar in the other, as if he was waiting for me. I was brave until I saw him, until I was facing his eyes, his hands, his big, fat, cruel self.

'What's that you've got, Bobby booby?' he said. 'A knife? Oh, Christ almighty, not *another* knife?' He laughed, but softly this time. 'Give it to me idiot. *Give.*'

It was like being in a web with the Fat as the spider. I could feel my fingers losing their strength round the hilt of the sheath-knife, but I gripped as hard as I could and said: 'I'm going to kill you.'

He just kept laughing and staring at me. I looked away from his eyes to get strong enough so that I could do what I meant to do, but that was worse, because I had to look at Mr. Summers then. He was still in the chair, but he wasn't sitting properly at all. He was all crumpled up and broken looking. There was no blood at all, no marks, but his face was very white and the strong electric light had made the silver pennies come over his eyes. He looked like something that had been used up and thrown away. He looked empty.

I rushed at the Fat then, but I couldn't see him because I was crying and I tripped and fell over the desk. I felt the knife being taken from me and then the Fat must have hit me, because everything went red, then nothing.

7: The Web

When I woke up I was still in the Fat's web. We were in the back of his car, locked in, and between the Fat, who was driving, and Mr. Summers and me, there was a glass screen. I tried to break it once but it was very strong glass and I could see the Fat laughing although I couldn't hear him.

Mr. Summers was breathing with little, whistly breaths and he never moved or spoke. I think he was broken inside from the Fat punching him. Every time I looked at him, I cried till I was all dried up and nothing else would come. I loved Mr. Summers.

Sometimes I slept, but not for very long at a time, and each time I woke it was the same. We were driving along in the country somewhere, going very fast, nothing outside the windows but darkness or sometimes the lights of another car. I was in the web and the web was moving. It carried us on and on until the dawn came and the light grew. Soon after this I began to recognize things. There were the prickly bushes with yellow flame-flowers and sometimes I caught a glimpse of high-banked lanes like the ones in Cornwall. The houses flicking past grew fewer and fewer until we were right out in the country, and I knew it was Cornwall when I saw the white-clay mountains in the distance, and I was glad and sorry at the same time.

Once we stopped in a big village and the Fat went to eat I think. He left us locked in the car of course, but I tried to attract somebody's attention by tapping at the window. Nobody came except a big black dog. He put his paws against the glass and I'm sure he would have helped us if he could, he looked like a good dog.

Then the Fat came back wiping his mouth, he kicked at the dog and it ran away. Oh, why don't people help you when you really need help?

I tried to make Mr. Summers comfortable, but there wasn't much I could do. His head hung forward and he would have fallen if I hadn't kept holding him back against the seat. I saw a rat like that once, with its head drooping down, down. I was with Mr. Summers in a lane when we found it just standing there, and it didn't run away, it couldn't, because it was dying. We waited until it finally fell down and then we buried it, but it took a long time to die. Mr. Summers told me it had been poisoned.

Now Mr. Summers was sagging and drooping just like the rat. Mr. Summers was dying.

Then there was the sun, and I knew it was going to be a lovely day. We drove on, still going very fast, and suddenly I saw the cliffs and the sea and I knew we were home. Everything was still clear in my head so that I could tell when we came near to our place. Then we passed near the beach where I had met Mr. Whiteside and the Fat slowed the car. The glass between us slid down and he said: 'Where do we go from here, booby? I know your place must be somewhere around. Show me which way to go.'

'I won't show you, I won't.'

The car stopped at the side of the road and the Fat lit a cigar, then he turned round to look at us.

'Maybe I should ask *Mr.* Summers?'

That was all he said, but I knew what he meant. I had to show him. It was funny, before all the trouble began I wouldn't have been able to find the valley very easily by myself, and I told you about the time when I couldn't find it at all, I suppose that was because I just followed Mr. Summers and didn't have to worry about it. But now that the Fat was here I had to find it. It was lucky my head was so clear.

I nodded and we set off again. By watching very carefully I was able to tell the Fat where to turn off on to the smaller road, and then we trundled down the lanes looking for the one which led to our valley. I made a mistake more than once and the Fat swore terribly. I think he was angry because the prickly bushes were scratching the sides of his big car. Then I found the right lane. It was much longer than I remembered it, and so narrow that the big car had to tilt up on the bank sometimes to get through. I told him when we came to the path and the first thing I heard when the car stopped was the swishing of the bamboo. It said, I wish, I wish, I wish –

I wished things. I wished the Fat would go away and leave us alone. I wished Mr. Summers would get better so that it could all be as it was before, so that we could go on with the work. But wishing isn't a real thing, the real things were getting out of the car and trying to get Mr. Summers out without hurting him. The real thing was walking up the path supporting, almost carrying Mr. Summers with the Fat rumbling along behind. The real things were bad things.

We went through the gate and past the bamboo and on to the door of the hut. Then I had to find the keyring in one of Mr. Summers' pockets with the Fat cursing behind me and telling me to hurry up for Christ's sake. We went in and the Fat kicked the door shut behind him. I laid Mr. Summers on his bed, on top of his sleeping bag, and sat by him. He was still breathing in little whistles, but not so loudly now and his eyes were closed. I don't really know what to do with sick people, so I just sat by him holding his hand, you can always sit and hold somebody's hand, you don't have to be clever to do that.

The Fat was so heavy that he made the hut shake as he walked about kicking things. He liked to kick things I think. He kicked the beds and the table and the chairs and everything.

'What a dump, Bobby booby. What a flaming dump.' He found the cupboard then. 'Make me some coffee, and hurry up, you dim bastard!'

I made the coffee on the primus stove in the kitchen as quickly as I could. Mr. Summers had shown me how to work the stove and I was quite good at it. I tried to get some of the coffee past Mr. Summers' lips, but I couldn't, it all just ran down his chin. The Fat laughed, then he tasted his own coffee and swore. He threw it at me and went over to the cupboard again, pulling everything out on to the floor until he found Mr. Summers' whisky.

'This is better, booby,' he said. He poured a lot into a glass and drank it in one go, then he came over and stood looking at Mr. Summers for a while.

'It's dead,' he said. 'Have we got a spade, idiot?'

Mr. Summers was *dead*. I touched his face and it was cold. Mr. Summers was dead! I cried then. I pushed my face into his coat and cried and cried, but he was still dead when I had finished.

'I said, have we got a spade, you blubbering little bastard?'

'What for?' I said.

'You'll have to bury it, that's what for. Do you know how to do that, or are you too thick even to dig a hole?'

'I know how to bury things,' I said.

The Fat looked at me funny for a moment from behind his cigar smoke. '*Do* you now, Bobby booby? Where is the spade?'

I told him there was one outside by the lavatory behind

the hut. He went out to get it and locked the door behind him. I was left alone with Mr. Summers for a minute or so, and I kissed his face. I don't know if you're supposed to do that to dead people, but I wanted Mr. Summers to know. Then the Fat came back and stood in the doorway with the spade in his hand.

'Get a move on,' he said.

Mr. Summers wasn't very heavy. I carried him outside and laid him down near the bamboo. Then I went back and got his sleeping bag, and though it was difficult I managed to get him into it. I pulled the strings at the end of it tight over his head so that he was all inside the bag, and then I began to dig. Digging with a spade is much harder than with a trowel, and I had to make a much bigger hole than I usually did. I dug it deep in the soft, black soil by the bamboo until the soil stopped and yellow clay began. I got blisters on my hands but I kept going. I wanted to make a good job of burying Mr. Summers. I loved Mr. Summers.

The sun was hot, especially when I got down so deep that the breeze couldn't get at me to cool me, and I thought about all sorts of things while I was digging. I could hear the sea-sound, making me think how big the sea must be and how small I was. It seemed that I couldn't really matter since I was so small. Then I thought about the birds and the little animals. They were even smaller than me so they couldn't matter much either. But they *did* matter, they mattered to me and they had mattered to Mr. Summers. Poor Mr. Summers.

Then I thought that after the birds and the animals there were the fishes, and after them the insects, and after them there were even smaller things, though I didn't know what they were called. Then there were trees and plants and grass and they were all *alive*, they all mattered. So I thought maybe I did too, and for a little while I felt a bit better. Then the hole was finished, as deep as I could make it because I had come to rocks. I climbed out and there was the Fat sitting on a chair which he must have brought out of the house. He looked sleepy, but I knew he was watching me.

I slid Mr. Summers down into the hole and laid him flat on the bottom, then I began to shovel the earth back, first the yellow clay and then the black soil until I had filled the hole in. I tramped about on it afterwards, and when I had finished nobody would have known that Mr. Summers was under there by the bamboo. Nobody except me and the Fat. I was very tired and my hands were hurting me, so I sat down on the ground to rest.

'What are you stopping for, Bobby booby?' the Fat said.

I said: 'Because I've finished.'

'Not yet,' he said. 'You have to dig another hole just like that one.' He pointed to a place a little farther away from the bamboo. 'Get digging.'

I began again like he told me to, but I was tired. I dug much more slowly than before, and I was working this time without thinking. I had got down to the yellow clay before I realised what I was doing. I was digging my own hole.

He came and stood over me as I worked, then after a while he dropped the end of his cigar into the hole at my feet.

'That's enough,' he said. 'Come into the house, I want a drink.'

I climbed out again and laid the shovel by the edge of the hole. He pushed me in front of him into the hut, but he left the door open this time. 'Sit,' he said, and I went over and sat on my bed. He poured whisky and drank and then again and again. I was afraid. I had always been afraid when

I was alone with the Fat, but now it was so much worse. I knew what was going to happen, and in a way I was glad. I only wished he would hurry up, then I would be out there with Mr. Summers under the bamboo and there wouldn't be any more Fat or any more anything.

He took one more drink of whisky before he took the knives from his pocket. There was the little one which Mr. Summers had brought along with him to the store and there was the big, shiny one which I had taken from the sports department. He laid the little knife down on the table and grasped the big knife in his fist. I had always hated his hands, they were bad hands. Now the blade of the knife stuck out from all those fingers he seemed to have, silver against the gold of his rings, and it looked like a tooth. One big, sharp tooth made of silver.

He stood up.

Then there was a noise, and it was so quiet in the hut that the noise seemed very loud. I wasn't frightened of the noise, but I think the Fat was. He whirled round to see where it was coming from. Do you know what it was?

You'll never guess.

It was a hedgehog. A big, old hedgehog walking in through the open door. It made a kind of scraping noise as it waddled along, and it kept on coming straight to me. I like hedgehogs.

The Fat was sweating and his face had gone red. He was *afraid*. The Fat was afraid!

I started to laugh, I just couldn't help it. People don't usually laugh when somebody is going to kill them, but I did. I said: 'You don't have to be afraid of a little hedgehog. Look, you can lift them if you don't touch the spines.'

I took it up very carefully the way Mr. Summers had shown me, but I couldn't stop laughing. The Fat looked so stupid with his face all red and sweating, he was just a big, fat man with a knife, that was all. And he looked so funny.

'Stop laughing, you stupid bastard! Stop laughing and put that bloody thing down!'

I could only shake my head, I was laughing so much that I couldn't speak. It was as if I was seeing the Fat for the first time, and everything was so clear in my head that I could even see through his clothes. I could see what his big, fat belly would be like, all wobbling and funny, and I could see what a big bum he had. I laughed until my throat hurt and my eyes began to water, and all the time his face got redder and redder and the sweat was running down his nose and dripping off the end! It was so *funny*.

Then he roared something at me, it wasn't words, it was more like the way the big animals speak. He rushed at me and poked at the hedgehog with the knife until it dropped out of my hands and rolled itself into a ball on the floor. The Fat went mad then. He grabbed the broom which was standing in a corner and beat and beat at the hedgehog until it was just a dead mess on the floor. The broom was broken and he threw it away and sat down in a chair. He was out of breath and he sat down so heavily that the chair creaked and for a moment I thought it would break and he would fall and I would start laughing again. But it didn't break, and he didn't fall, and I didn't laugh.

The Fat wasn't funny any more.

He poured some whisky and drank it. He drank until the bottle was empty and then he threw it at me, but it missed and smashed against the wall behind me. He got up again.

'Now, you little bastard –'

The sun shining through the window made the knife glitter like silver, like a coin.

Money!

I remembered the money and suddenly I knew I had a chance to live. When I knew I had the chance I *wanted* to live.

'There's a lot of money,' I said. 'I know where there's an awful lot of money.'

The knife hung in front of my face like a hawk, then it lowered and the Fat stepped back.

'What money? Where?'

'The money Mr. Summers hid,' I said. 'It's a lot of money.'

'Idiot,' the Fat said, but I knew he loved money. He said: 'How much money do you think there is booby? Fifty quid? A hundred?' He was laughing at me. 'I suppose you think a hundred is a lot?'

He lifted the knife again. 'It'll take more than a measly hundred to save you now, you loathsome little prick.'

'It's thousands,' I said. 'Thousands and thousands and *thousands*.'

He was wondering, I could see him wondering about it. He put the big knife in his pocket and sat down at the table again. After a while he lit a cigar and just sat looking, looking right into me to see if I was telling the truth.

'Show me this money,' he said.

'You won't hurt me then?' I asked him. 'Promise you won't?'

'We'll see, Bobby my booby, we'll see.'

'No, no, you've got to promise,' I said.

He took the knife out of his pocket and sort of played with it. 'I don't make promises to half-wits like you. Show me where it is.'

'All right,' I said, 'but put the knife away first.'

'Don't worry about the knife, Bobby,' he said. He was pushing the fat about on his face to make it smile, and he had called me Bobby, not idiot or bastard or Bobby booby. That meant he was getting excited about the money, it meant I might have a chance yet.

The cupboard was a good bit lighter since the Fat had emptied all the food out on to the floor, and I managed to push it aside quite easily. I knew which board was the loose one and I prised it up with the handle of a teaspoon. He came over and threw me aside so that I fell across my bed. I watched him bending over to look under the floor. He swore softly and went down on his knees to reach for the first box. It was awkward to get to in there, but he stretched and puffed until his face and neck got red and he got it. After he found the right key on Mr. Summers' keyring and opened the box the money was in his hands, wads and wads of money and he got more red in the face and more excited until I think he forgot about me. I got up from the bed and tried to slip away, but the floor creaked and he looked up.

'Where do you think you're going?'

'Nowhere,' I said. 'There's more under there.'

'More?'

'Another two boxes,' I said. 'Farther in under the floor.'

He said Christ then and put the first box down, but to get to where the other two boxes were he had to stretch his arm right underneath the floorboards, which was easy for thin, little people like me and Mr. Summers, but not for someone as fat as the Fat. His neck bulged red against his white collar and he grunted and cursed.

I was near the table and on the table lay Mr. Summers' little knife. I could have run away then I think, he was too busy to notice. But I had a better idea. I picked up the little knife and stood over the Fat. I wanted to kill him but I didn't know where you have to stick a knife to kill somebody, so I just drew its edge across the big, red sausage between the place where his collar ended and the place where his hair began.

Blood came out and he screamed. I didn't think his big, heavy voice could sound so thin and high up. And the blood. I didn't really expect that to come and turn his white collar red. I wouldn't have been surprised if some kind of white, squodgy stuff had oozed out of him, but not *blood*, not from the Fat.

I ran then. Out of the hut and across the garden, past the bamboo and up the path. I passed his car in the lane and ran down towards the sea, and all the time I could hear the Fat roaring. I knew he would come after me if he could, but I wasn't really afraid. I could run much faster than him, and anyway, he was bleeding. But I *am* stupid and I *did* make a mistake even then. I had chosen to run down the narrow lane towards the sea, and that was the direction his car was pointing. If I had gone up the lane he couldn't have used the car because it was too narrow there for him to turn it round, and beside, it's harder to make a car go backwards than forwards I think.

I heard the engine start up just as the lane began to climb again. Mr. Summers and I had never come this way before, we always went up to the road in the mornings so I didn't know what was in front of me. I was surprised when the lane began to go uphill, up towards the cliffs. Gradually the high bank on either side fell away, leaving a bare, stony track which seemed to be going nowhere at all. I climbed up it as fast as I could but I couldn't run very well going uphill. Then I was at the clifftop and there was a castle.

I was so surprised to see a castle that I forgot to be afraid for a moment. It was a funny looking place, all ruined and made of huge blocks of stone. A sort of tower rose high into the sky and the ground about the place was awful to walk on, nothing but sharp stones which hurt my feet as I ran over them. The Fat's car was close now, almost at the top of the hill, so I ran to hide in the ruined castle.

As I went in two birds flew out, they were black with greyish heads, jackdaws I think, then I looked through a kind of window in the stonework and saw the big black and silver car come over the rise.

8: The Hole

He stopped the car on the stones in front of the castle. I think he was afraid. He was afraid of *me*. I didn't even have the little knife any more, I had dropped it in the hut after I cut him, but he was afraid to leave his car.

It was like a game of hide and seek where I could see the Fat but he couldn't see me. He was all bloody. There was blood on his face and neck, and in his hair and over his shoulders and down the front of his shirt. He had his hands on the steering wheel and they had got covered in blood as well. I suppose he must have had an awful lot of blood in him, being such a big man I mean. Even from a distance I could see his eyes and they looked twice as big and blue as before. They were bulging out, darting everywhere at once, looking for *me*.

I went out of the other side of the square part of the castle where he couldn't see me. There was a metal plate fixed to the wall outside, it said: THE WHEAL HIGH MINE. NATIONAL TRUST.

It wasn't a castle, it was a mine! And the tower was only a rotten old chimney. That was a disappointment to me, but it *looked* like a castle with all those big stones and everything. To my right there was a fence, a square fence round a big hole. I wanted to go and have a look down the hole, but I couldn't because the Fat would have been able to see me then.

He still had the engine running in his car. It was giving frightened little grunts every so often, and when it did that it moved an inch or two forward each time. I picked up a sharp, heavy stone and slipped round the mine-building.

When he wasn't looking in my direction I stepped out and threw the stone at the car and hid myself again quickly. Instead of smashing through as I had hoped, the stone just made a white star come on the surface of the glass so that I couldn't see his face any more.

Some big white gulls came down from the sky over the sea and screamed above the mine-building, they must have seen what I had done because they sounded excited. I threw more stones until the whole of the glass in the front of the Fat's car was like a sheet of white sugar crystals, so he couldn't see out at all. I danced out into the open then, because I knew the Fat wouldn't get out of the car. He was *afraid*. The gulls saw me dancing and got more and more excited, swooping down low to the ground almost calling to me. I called back to them and laughed and the sun came out. I smashed the headlights of the Fat's car with more stones, and I made big dents in the body of it as well, but he still didn't come out. It was going all right, everything was going all right!

I shouted at the Fat: 'Fat, Fat, Fat!' I sang: 'The Fat's afraid, the Fat's afraid –'

Then I looked up into the sun and it exploded in my face. The terrible fire filled my head and I fell. The sharp stones cut my hands and knees as I hit the ground. I was having one of my fits.

Away deep down at the bottom of the fire in my head there was a cool place where I was all right. I looked out from that cool place and saw myself lying there on the stones having one of my stupid fits because I'd got too excited, and I was angry with myself. I fought the flames inside my head from that cool place until the coolness spread and got bigger and I began to win. I *made* the fit go away. I'd never done that before, the fits had always seemed too strong to fight against, but now I had made it go away. Without pills or people to help me or anything. I did it by myself.

A sharp sound startled me and I looked up. I'd forgotten about the Fat. He was smashing the sugary glass of the window from the inside, hitting it hard with something heavy. He made a jagged hole like a hole in ice and then I could see his face. It was a horrible face.

There was blood to start with, and his skin had gone a funny grey colour. The whole of his face seemed to have melted. It was the wrong shape. It was no shape at all, and staring from this were the eyes. They widened when he saw me lying there by the fence in front of the hole. The car's engine screamed, the way the Fat had screamed when I cut him, and then it roared as he had roared and rushed forward at me very fast.

Sometimes, when you're very happy or very afraid, a little piece of time can stretch out like elastic so that it seems like a very long time. That was one of those elastic times. Everything was so slow.

I rolled over away from the car, once, twice, three times I rolled, and although I knew the sharp stones must be hurting me I didn't feel them at all. It was like rolling in the air, and I felt so light, as if I hadn't any body to hold me to the ground. The car was the same. It looked much bigger than it had been before, big enough to fill the sky above me, and it was so *slow*. It hit me then, not hard, but just enough to push me farther away, and everything snapped back to its proper speed just like a piece of elastic as I said.

I heard the car squeal again, as if it was afraid, and then there was the Fat's voice shouting something. It must have hit the fence then, because I heard a snapping, crunching noise and then a slipping sound and then nothing for a while except a loud banging that got less and less until it was very far away. Then silence.

I turned my head to see what had happened to the car, but there wasn't any car. Or any fence. The car had gone down the hole. I wanted to see, but when I tried to get up I fell down again, so I crawled to the edge of the hole. It seemed a long way over the sharp stones and the sun was so hot that I could feel my scalp all wet and prickly. I was nearly within arm's reach of the edge when I saw the Fat, or rather I saw his hands. They were more like spiders than ever, red, bloody spiders, with the fingers wriggling and digging into the black earth as they tried to pull the Fat up. I watched the red spiders for a long time, but they couldn't pull the Fat up. He was too heavy you see, much too heavy.

The gulls were still above us, diving and crying all the time. One of them landed just beside me and walked in that funny way that they do until it was between me and the Fat and I couldn't see his hands any more. I tried to remember what the proper name for that kind of gull was. It was one of those very big ones, the white, clean looking ones that don't look big when they're flying, but look really enormous when you see them sitting or walking about close to you.

I tried and tried to remember its name, but I couldn't. I wished I had had my bird book with me, then I could have said its name all right. It stood staring at me for a while before it walked on past me, and then I looked at the place where the Fat's hands had been, but there was nothing. Just nothing. The Fat was down the hole.

*

I must have slept for a while then, and when I woke the gulls were gone. I lay where I was remembering all that had happened. I thought about things very carefully, and then I knew what I had to do.

The fence wasn't really broken, but three of the wooden posts had been pulled up out of the ground and the wire had snapped in two places. I cleaned out the post holes with my hands and stood the posts upright in them again. I hammered them down with a big stone and packed earth and stones around them until they were firm and strong. The broken wire was more difficult, but I found some old bits of wire inside the mine-building and I managed to repair it with them. When I was finished and had made the wires tight and straight as before, you would never have known that a car had gone through the fence and down the hole. Everything was almost exactly as it had been before. The last thing I did was to wipe out the wheelmarks that the Fat's car had made. I scraped them away with a stone right up to the edge of the hole, and I looked down the hole. There was nothing there but blackness and quiet. I dropped a stone down and after a long time I thought I heard it hit the bottom, but it was a watery, faint kind of sound. It was an awful long way down.

I came away from there then and started to walk back to the track which would lead me to the hut. I was sore all over and a cold wind had started to blow in from the sea. I looked back at the mine-building and the hole with the fence round it, and it was all just as it had been when I first saw it. I still thought it looked like a castle. I supposed that some of the holiday people would come to look at it, but not many, it was too far from the road and the hole was a bit frightening when you went too close to it. So nobody would ever know what had happened except me and the gulls, and I wasn't going to tell anybody.

I went on down the track. It was getting colder and I wanted a nice cup of tea.

*

I had to clean the hut up when I got back before I could have my tea. There was all the mess the Fat had made with his blood, and there was the money to put back in its secret place and all the food to put back in the cupboard again. Some of it had blood on it and I had to throw it away. I put all the rubbish out into the big hole I had dug for myself and then filled it in. I put the hedgehog that the Fat had killed in there too. It was an awful big hole for a hedgehog to be buried in, but I didn't want to do any more digging. Not even a little hole with my trowel.

When the place was clean I had my tea and went to bed early. I was really tired, too tired even to dream.

*

I'm all right now. I live in the hut by myself and do the work. At first I was sad every time I passed the bamboo and the place where Mr. Summers is buried, but gradually it began to seem as if the bamboo *was* Mr. Summers and when I hear it swishing in the wind I feel happy because Mr. Summers is so near. The summer is almost over now and there are fewer cars on the roads, but there's been an awful lot of work to do. I've taken my sleeping bag and some food and stayed out working for days and days together. I'm getting good at finding the secret places to sleep in and I know all the different kinds of birds and plants and flowers now. When I'm back in the hut it's all right, too, I know how to work the primus stove and everything and I can eat all the things I like. But it's beginning to get a little bit lonely now that the winter is on the way and the darkness comes sooner.

I went into the town last week to buy myself a woolly jumper to keep out the cold, and while I was there I bought a transistor radio. That helps a little, I can even take it with me when I'm walking the lanes, it's very small. But it's not really the same as having someone with you.

I don't want another *person* here though, because I don't think there could be anyone else like Mr. Summers, but there's a pet shop in town and sometimes they have puppies in the window. I've got plenty of money, so I think I'll get a puppy the next time I go there. I think about the store sometimes and wonder what will happen to it. It's mine really, but I don't want it, I just want to stay here and do the work. I'm in charge of all the work now you see, and sometimes I get worried that I won't be able to manage it all by myself. When I get like that I go out and sit by the bamboo where Mr. Summers is and then everything seems to come all right again.

I never go up to the old mine-building any more. I went once, but I got frightened when I looked down the hole where the Fat is with his car.

Everything is nice when I'm out working, especially when the sun is shining, but sometimes when the wind blows at night from the sea and it's dark outside I get scared. I don't know what it is I'm afraid of, because the Fat's dead and dead people don't come back, but I'm always glad when morning comes.

It'll be better when I have a dog, a good, big dog. Maybe I'll even get two dogs.

Out of the blue . . .

INDIGO

the best in modern writing